SPELLCASTER HIDDEN

SPELLBOUND SHIFTERS: FATES & VISIONS BOOK THREE

KEIRA BLACKWOOD

LIZA STREET

ALSO BY KEIRA BLACKWOOD & LIZA STREET

Spellbound Shifters: Dragons Entwined

Dragon Forgotten

Dragon Shattered

Dragon Unbroken

Dragon Reborn

Dragon Ever After

Spellbound Shifters: Fates & Visions

Oracle Defiant

Oracle Adored

Spellcaster Hidden

Spellbound Shifters Standalones

Hope Reclaimed

Orphan Entangled

ALSO BY KEIRA BLACKWOOD

The Protectors of Sawtooth Peaks

Running to the Pack

Defending the Pack

Uniting the Pack

Howl with the Pack

Leaving the Pack

The Protectors of the Pack

Bodyguard

Enemies

Heir

Warrior

Scoundrel

The Protectors of Riverwood

Grizzly Bait

Grizzly Mate

Grizzly Fate

The Protectors Unlimited

Can't Prove Shift

Suave as Shift

In Deep Shift

The Protectors Quick Bites (with Eva Knight)

Midnight Wish

I Dream of Grizzly

The Ocean's Roar

To Catch a Werewolf

Outfoxed

Tactics & Tails

The Vampires of Scarlet Harbor

Pierced

Hunted

Ruled

Alphas & Alchemy: Elemental Shifters (with Eva Knight)

Dragon Guardian of Land

ALSO BY LIZA STREET

The Sierra Pride

Fierce Wanderer

Fierce Heartbreaker

Fierce Protector

Fierce Player

Fierce Dancer

Fierce Informer

Fierce Survivor

Fierce Lover

The Corona Pride

Savage Yearning

Savage Loss

Savage Heartache

Savage Thirst

Savage Bliss

Savage Redemption

Savage Penance

The Dark Pines Pride

Wild Homecoming

Wild Atonement

Wild Reunion

Wild Engagement

The Rock Creek Clan

The Rose King

Ruthless Misfit

Ruthless Outlaw

Ruthless Fighter

Ruthless Rogue

This is a work of fiction. Any resemblance to any actual persons, places, or events is coincidental. All characters in this story are at least 18 years of age or older.

The cover utilizes stock images licensed by the author. The model(s) depicted have no connection to this work or any other work by the author.

CHAPTER 1

With no idea where I was headed, I held tight to the steering wheel and hit the gas. Well, I had *some* idea of where I was going. The highway said west, so I knew that much.

Ten months had gone by since last Thanksgiving, when I'd left everything behind. Months on the road, hiding out in the woods, mostly sleeping in my car. Shifting into my wolf form to kill a rabbit every few days. Not too often, because I felt guilty every time. I always picked an old one at the end of its life, but it would be so much easier to just slap down my credit card and order a cheeseburger at a fast food joint.

Easier, yeah. But dangerous. Credit cards could be tracked.

The world whizzed past, trees and fields blending together in a puke-green blur dulled by the setting sun.

Chad Curtis had held me prisoner, but I was a prisoner no more. Still, this world outside wasn't safe. The trees and fields outside my window could be concealing my enemies. People who wanted to use me as a tool for their own gain.

I was just a girl, though. An obedient daughter, a sweet

sister. Yes, I was a powerful oracle, but my powers hadn't been working so well since my escape.

When I'd been locked up in Chad Curtis's tower, stuck in that cell, I'd known a rescue was coming, just like I had known it was time to leave Emerald Pines after that rescue. Visions of the future had always been a gift, until it was a curse. And then the visions, my powers seemed to break...or maybe *I* broke.

A sign up ahead said the next town was Marisol, sixteen miles away. That name...I knew I hadn't been here before. I'd never been to Pennsylvania, but there was something about the name Marisol that sparked recognition. It was right there in my head, I was sure of it, but I couldn't remember what about.

A flash of black crossed my vision, a sledgehammer to my head. I tried to blink it away, but this is what my visions had become since the cell. Uncontrollable, unpredictable. Useless.

Now I knew what Sparrow felt like. She'd never been able to master her visions. Although, from my last vision-correspondence with her, it seemed like she was getting more of a handle on it.

She'd told me I was in danger and I needed to leave Emerald Pines. Something I already knew, thank you very much, after being freaking *kidnapped*.

She'd also said something about *mates*, plural. But I must have heard her wrong.

The road appeared in front of me once more. I exhaled and relaxed my grip on the steering wheel. This was fine, I could do this.

A sign flickering in and out of existence up ahead was my only warning—the road in front of me wasn't real. I slammed on the brakes, forcing my body to behave in the physical world while my mind took me somewhere else.

A vision of driving *while* driving? That was messed up.

My sister, Sparrow, appeared on the side of the road. A wave of darkness swirled around her and she hunched her body against it. The darkness pressed in on her, and I called out, reaching forward as if I could touch her through the windshield.

The vision flickered to nothing, and I caught the flash of a honeybee glinting in the sunlight. I knew it wouldn't make sense to puzzle it out now; my visions didn't work like that, so I watched instead as the vision played out.

The bee transformed into darkness once more. With a powerful sucking sound, that wave of darkness left my sister.

And flew straight for me.

The brakes squealed and I felt the ground go uneven beneath the rental car's tires. Crap. Crap, crap, crap, I was off the road, while in front of me, my vision was showing a smooth drive. In reality, I could be headed straight into a tree.

Panicked, I wanted to yank the steering wheel. But one way or the other could send me into danger.

The car slowed over jagged ditches, jostling me up and down. My entire body was tense, even though it made the jostling hurt more. I braced myself for a crash that never came.

As soon as the car stopped, my vision went away. Figured. In its place, it left a pounding headache and the taste of metal on my tongue. I'd bitten my lip at some point.

I'd never had a vision like that before, never one where I knew something was going to happen to me. They were always about someone else. It worked that way for both me and my sister. Something terrible was coming.

I looked through the windshield, grateful to be able to see in front of me again. The bumper of the car seemed to be about an inch from a towering evergreen.

I climbed out of the car and leaned against it, catching my breath. The tires had gone into a final, jagged ditch. The ditch made no sense—it was like a big old moat had been dug along the side of the road. A series of them, actually.

Puzzled, I reached out to one of them. A flare of energy met my hand, burning white with magic.

Holy crap. I'd driven straight into a witch's wards. It explained the series of ditches—whoever this witch was, she'd probably filled them with whatever medium she excelled at. Salt, blood, or ash. I peered closer. Flakes of ash were scattered around, as well as chunks of salt. Blood wouldn't be visible unless it was fresh, but from the power infused in the ward, I had to guess it was.

All three had been used.

I threw my hand one way, and encountered the flare of energy above another ditch. Then I moved a hand back, behind me.

I was trapped between two wards.

It didn't make sense that I'd been able to drive through them. I should have crashed, or been repelled.

The sign from my vision popped into my head again, not as a vision, but a memory. I squinted my mind's eye, struggling to see the words. *Spellbound Academy*. How had I ended up here?

More importantly, how would I get out of these wards?

I pushed against the magical barrier in front of me again, testing it. My hand met energy that was so hard, it felt like a solid wall.

No one was around. I hadn't seen another car in ages. Was I going to be stuck between these barriers forever?

"To hell with that shit," I muttered, then I smiled—I sounded exactly like my sister.

If the ditches were any indication, the ward in front of me was the last one, and then I'd be in the woods. From there, I could find whatever witch—or witches, rather, now that I knew I was at an academy—had set up the wards, and I could ask them to kindly free my car and I would be on my merry way.

Or...would I?

What better place to hide from those who sought me, than a secret academy?

My magic was just as strong as my mother's, if not stronger, because I had shapeshifter blood from my father. Unfortunately, I wasn't trained to be a witch; I'd just learned a few things here and there from Mom.

Still, I could see the energies weaving together to create the ward. If I could identify the individual strands, I could tease them apart, separate them.

I unfocused my gaze, using my witch's sight to better see what I was working with.

I didn't know how long I stood there, slowly pulling apart the different strands of energy, before I had a hole in the ward large enough to step through.

Turning, I gave my car a final glance. There wasn't much inside it, and maybe I'd come back for it later, once I figured out a way to stay here.

I stepped through the hole I'd made in the ward, then let go of the edges. The energies snapped back into place.

Was that what I'd done earlier, with my car? It hadn't felt like it. I shrugged. I didn't understand magic—maybe I'd never know how I got in.

More importantly, I faced what looked like a never-ending forest. There was no sign of an academy here, or even of another person. But if I kept walking, I'd come to the school or someone else eventually. At least, that's what I told myself in order to be brave enough to make my way through the forest.

My little slip-ons had not been made for treks through

the woods. I thought of shifting to my wolf, letting her take the lead. My wolf would be more comfortable here than I was. But if I met someone, and I was sure to meet someone eventually, I told myself, then I'd want to be able to talk to them and explain why I was here.

Human form it was.

Evening was coming on. The sun had dipped below the treetops, and it gave the forest a spooky feel. A noise reached my ears, a kind of snuffling growl.

I froze in my tracks, alert to danger. I scented the air, but there was nothing but cool autumn forest. Holding my breath, I peered through the tree trunks ahead of me.

A creature burst forth—a humanoid monster twice my height. It had leathery gray skin like an elephant's, a single eye, and stood on two legs. Its mouth was open in a grotesque grin that would've been funny if it hadn't been so terrifying.

I screamed and didn't think about anything—I turned around and blindly ran.

The monster was behind me, so close I could hear the sound of it panting. I risked a look to see how far away it was.

Big mistake.

Fingers outstretched, the monster reached for me. I ducked back behind a tree, but not fast enough. He snagged my foot and pulled. My back scraped across the ground and I tried to keep my head up as I frantically searched for any advantage. *There.* I grabbed the trunk of a sapling for dear life. The monster stumbled and his grip loosened just enough to free my ankle, though he did catch my shoe.

My body flopped down to the ground and I scrambled away as quickly as I could. I'd been wrong. Human form *was not* for the best. I needed some space so I could shift without being grabbed again. Back on my feet, I ran, weaving through the trees. I'd never run so fast as a human.

Debris cut my bare ankle, sharp rocks and sticks cutting the bottom of my foot. Each step hurt more than the last until my whole leg was numb. But I didn't stop, I didn't slow. I needed more distance, I needed more time, but the monster was gaining on me.

The hair on the back of my neck prickled with the feel of the monster's hot breath. It smelled like rot and forest, like blood.

No, the blood was mine.

It ensnared me, huge hands crushing my chest. There was no time left. I called to the wolf inside of me, shifting in a glow of white light.

The monster let go, dropping me to the ground. I didn't look back to see its reaction, and instead I took my advantage. Still tangled in my clothes, I ran.

Snarls came from behind me, but there were no more footfalls, no more breathing down my neck. Instead, there was a sound I knew all too well, the sound of a wolf fighting. I stopped and turned.

Sure enough, a large gray wolf danced around the monster's legs, tearing at its ankles. No, not tearing, stringing some kind of glowing rope.

The monster reached down, swiping at the wolf. The wolf's body twisted, knocking the beast off balance, and it fell to the ground.

The wolf stepped away completely unharmed, and completely in control. He shifted back to human form. Hot damn, he was easily the best thing I'd ever seen. He was huge, the monster truck of men. If men were all cars, they'd be crushed by this guy with a single glance. He was over six feet of tanned skin and muscled perfection, with a hard look like he'd sooner punch someone than say hello. His hair was black and cropped short, and so was his beard. I wasn't entirely sure that he'd noticed me, since he didn't even look my way, but that might not have been the worst thing. Instead, he picked up his pants from the ground and pulled them on and found a black shirt, which he put on as well. Pity. Then he slid on a pair of sunglasses even though there was little sunlight left, and pulled a walkie from his belt.

"It's me," he said into the walkie. "Tell the chancellor someone's broken through the wards. They got far enough to wake one of the Guardians."

"Right away," a woman's voice replied. "How is that even possible?"

"I don't know, but the Guardian was more aggressive than usual. Something about this woman set it off."

Okay, so he had seen me.

"Did the Guardian finish the job?" the woman asked.

"No, the intruder still has her memories. She's in wolf form. The chancellor will want to talk with her."

"Bring her here immediately, Vosovich. The chancellor has an opening in her schedule."

I stood frozen, staring as the guy, Vosovich, lifted his head and met my gaze. Well, it seemed like he did, because his face was tilted toward me, but all I could see was the hard set of his jaw since he was wearing sunglasses.

He said, "I'll bring her right there."

Uh oh. That was what I'd wanted, right? To meet the witches in charge of this place? Watching the big man stalk toward me, I felt more like I'd been caught doing something wrong. Like I should get back to my car and forget this whole thing ever happened.

"You. Girl." He grabbed my pants and shoes from the ground and carried them toward me. "Come here."

I didn't have any pants. Taking a quick note of what was

still wrapped around my wolf body, I realized I at least hadn't lost my shirt and bra. But I had lost my underwear.

"I'm uh...good right here, thanks." Given he was also a wolf shifter, I knew he would understand the shifter tongue.

Vosovich tossed me my clothes.

"Turn around, please," I said. I'd never been afraid to be naked in front of other shifters. It was a natural part of shifting. But usually I was shifting in front of my pack. And this felt...more meaningful.

He did as I said without another word, and I shifted back to human form. I stared at his back, watching that he didn't turn around while I was getting dressed.

Once my shoes were on, I cleared my throat. "Okay. You can turn around."

He didn't. Instead, he started walking. "This way."

I waved a hand at the monster. "What about that?"

"The rope will disappear after a while. The Guardian will go back to the forest to do its job. Come on."

This was it, my last chance to run. I could go back to my car and wait for the trouble I'd seen in my vision to find me. I could find another ride and keep moving. Or, I could go into the academy, prove that I belonged here, and maybe I could even learn something in the process. My powers had always been intuitive, and I'd just figured them out as I went. But if I could harness them, learn *how* to see the magic and what I was supposed to do with it, well, maybe I wouldn't have to hide anymore.

I rushed to keep up, eyeing the man who'd helped me. He looked to be in his late twenties or early thirties, but for shifters, that could mean he was anywhere from twenty-five to fifty years old.

The woman on the walkie had called him Vosovich. I wondered what his job was here. Monster keeper? Grounds guardian? His scowl told me he wouldn't answer if I asked. So I followed him and didn't say a thing.

We pressed through the forest until the trees broke and I got my first glimpse of a castle I should have been able to see from the road. Dark stone spires reached up toward the sky, and when I stared at the structure, I couldn't help but feel like I'd done this before. It was the weirdest thing, like I'd dreamed of this place in vivid detail.

Vosovich led me to front doors. The ring handle lifted, the doors slowly opened, and we stepped inside. I looked back to see who had opened the doors that opened for us, but no one was there.

Even the scent of the school was vaguely familiar, a mix of old books and cool earth like a deep cave. There was an impossibly long rug along the floor, dusky blue like the evening sky. It led down an endless, empty hallway.

Maybe I should have been afraid, but I wasn't. Part of me knew I belonged here, and that I had nothing to fear from this place. Everything was well lit, like it was daytime in the summer back home on the family compound. But when I looked up, there were no light fixtures.

Vosovich turned down the first corridor we reached and took a seat in one of the blue chairs lined up along the wall. "Sit."

I took the chair beside him. Was he always so curt? Or was it just me? He probably wasn't thrilled about having to come to my rescue.

A short woman popped her head out of the office across from us. "The chancellor will see you now."

Suddenly, I was no longer so sure of my place here. Vosovich definitely didn't want me here, and the secretary wasn't welcoming at all. I'd have to do my damnedest to convince the chancellor I belonged.

CHAPTER 2

I stood on shaking legs. Vosovich reached over to catch me, but I waved him away. I didn't want his help, the sanctimonious grump. Besides, he'd already shown me that he didn't like me or want me here.

The red-haired secretary gave me a sympathetic smile, easing some of my worries. Then she sat down at a little wooden desk. I took a deep breath, ignored Vosovich, and approached the half-open door.

Kim Ellison, Chancellor read the plaque next to it. Why did I know that name?

I stepped inside her office and filled my nose with the scent of sage. There was no extra hint of wild animal, so I knew this woman wasn't a shifter. Not like the cranky wolf who was hot on my heels.

She sat behind her desk, her attention on a tablet in front of her. Her dark hair was pulled back into a no-nonsense bun, and a pair of rectangular reading glasses were perched on her nose. Before I could introduce myself, she stood and smoothed her skirt, then reached across the desk to take my hand.

"Welcome back," she said. "Please, sit."

Back? "Thank you." Maybe I'd come here when I was a kid or something. Maybe this was where my mother had gone to school. If it was, this woman appeared too young to have been the chancellor then.

Everything about this place was familiar, and yet not, like the weirdest case of déjà vu ever. I shot a glance at Vosovich, wondering if he'd leave to give us privacy to talk, but he remained in the room.

"Adrien," she said to him, "you may take a seat, as well."

Adrien, huh? It suited him. A blocky, handsome name for a blocky, handsome guy. He took a seat beside me, dominating the office with his giant stature. He even took off his sunglasses, revealing the most gorgeous set of brown eyes. There was a golden ring at the edge of his irises, a touch of light in the darkness.

"So," the chancellor said, "I'm Kim Ellison, and I make sure Spellbound Academy is running smoothly."

She waited, hands folded in front of her, for my response.

"I'm...Morgan," I said. It was a half-truth—Morgan was my mom's name and my middle name. It would work.

She shot me a look that said she knew I was lying. How could she know that? What was I missing?

"Professor Vosovich informed us that you not only tested our wards, but you got far enough—on your own—to wake one of our Guardians."

I shuddered at the memory of that beast. It had looked like something conjured from the pits of hell.

She continued, "Why, pray tell, were you attacking our wards?"

"I..." I didn't have a good answer, or any answer, really. "I promise, that wasn't what I was doing. I was just trapped between them."

She gave me a doubtful look.

"Really," I insisted.

I had never been a "bad girl." That was always Sparrow's role. I was the good one, the kid who obeyed everything Mom and Dad said, the teenager who didn't rebel. I'd quietly done everything I was told my entire life. But somehow, even if it seemed like I'd done the wrong thing, I knew I was supposed to be here. This time it wasn't because of a vision, but a feeling in my gut.

There was also that darkness I'd seen. The bee. There was a reason oracles didn't get visions about themselves, because they never knew how to react. Run? Hide? Fight? I didn't know. All I knew was that vision had freaked me the hell out, and I felt safer here.

The chancellor spoke again. "You don't remember the last time, do you, *Morgan?*"

"The last time what?" I was desperate, and confused, and beginning to get frustrated, though I kept my voice even.

"Interesting." The chancellor tapped her pen on the desk and narrowed her eyes at me. "You've been here before. A week ago you arrived at Spellbound Academy, walked right through our wards, and ended up sitting across from me in this office with Professor Vosovich, as we are now."

"That's...crazy." It was, wasn't it?

"We sent you away after our interview. Your memories were erased, which is why your return is so peculiar."

I felt Vosovich's gaze on me. His face softened just a little as he looked me over.

"Look," I said. "I don't know what you're talking about, but I need your help."

"I know. And the answer, this time, is yes."

So many questions were rattling around in my head, I didn't know which to ask first. "Why are you changing your mind?"

She steepled her fingers in front of her. "I can tell your

need is great, for one thing. But more importantly from the academy's interests is that if you're talented enough to break through our wards not only once, but then return to the school after a memory charm and break through a second time, then you're talented enough for Spellbound. Is that clear, Ms. Solaris?"

"How do you know my name...never mind." If we'd had this conversation before, she already knew my name and that I needed help. Or she knew I'd ask whether I could stay. Or… "To make sure we're on the same page, you know I want to stay here, right?"

The chancellor nodded. "I don't care who you're hiding from, and I have no interest in finding out. You're too important; we've never had someone break a memory charm before."

"Oh. Great."

The chancellor offered me her hand. "Welcome to Spellbound Academy, Morgan Rose."

"Rose?" I liked it—it sounded good with Morgan. But this whole situation was bonkers. I felt like I was imagining it. Dreaming it. Was this a vision?

"It's the alias you picked last time you came to my office."

"Okay, great."

"You'll find our wards will shield you from the outside world. That means it won't be possible for you to communicate telepathically with anyone while you're in attendance."

That meant I couldn't reach out to my sister. But, no one else would be able to find me. This was exactly what I needed —a shield while I figured out where I should go next.

"Classes started the first week of September, the day after you first arrived. Which means you're now a week late starting the semester. As a result, you won't have a choice in classes, and it'll be your responsibility to catch up on the work you've missed."

That hardly seemed fair, given that I would've been on time if they'd let me in when I first asked. Still, it didn't sound so bad. I'd work hard and learn everything I had to. My life depended on it.

The chancellor stood up, so I did the same. Whatever happened next, I'd found my safe place.

"Professor Vosovich will escort you to the dormitories," she said. "You will begin classes tomorrow."

"Thank you. I won't let you down."

"Just a reminder," she said, "your performance will determine your future here. This is a two-year university. Only the top fifty percent move on to the second year after the end of the first."

She ushered me out of the office with a firm but gentle hand on my shoulder. My thoughts lingered on her words. Fifty percent. That meant the other half had to leave. I couldn't let myself be in that half. I needed this.

The chancellor returned to her office, and it was just me and the big, burly wolf shifter standing alone in the hall.

"This way." He started walking without waiting for me. I hurried to keep up, but he kept himself a few steps ahead.

My mind was spinning. I was sure there were a million questions I should have been asking, but I couldn't think of any of them. Vosovich probably wouldn't answer me anyway.

We went down a long corridor and up two flights of stairs. Everything was stone and wood and plaster, classic like a castle kept exactly the same for hundreds of years.

Vosovich smelled good—good in a way that made me want to walk a little closer to him, let my shoulder brush against his arm. I felt drawn to him, and it was pissing me off.

"Did you know I was here before?" I asked him.

He flicked his dark gaze to me and nodded once.

"Did you make me leave?" I asked.

"I was there, yeah."

I frowned at him. I hated the thought that there were memories lost, ideas and conversations I might never get back.

"Where are we going?" I asked him.

"To see the hall director, Maxwell. He'll find you a room, get you settled."

Maxwell...I'd met a Maxwell, once. Sexy dragon shifter.

We walked in silence for a couple more minutes.

"I don't have my bag," I said, "or any of my clothes."

"They're in your car?" he asked.

I nodded.

"Give me your keys. I'll get them for you."

I handed him my key ring. "Thanks."

Sounds of laughter and music reached my ears, coming from around a corner. Vosovich and I rounded it, and the dark, solid hallway of closed doors transformed into a place of light and music. Doorways lined this hall, but every door was open, save for one.

It was the closed door that Vosovich led me to. We paused outside of it.

"Listen," Vosovich said. "Morgan."

"Wren," I whispered.

"What?"

"That's my name." I didn't know why I'd told him. A part of me wanted to be closer. Give him a piece of me, a secret.

"You can't tell anyone that," he said. "I don't know exactly what kind of danger you're in, but you *must* keep it a secret."

"Okay." I looked down.

"Listen," he said.

"Yeah?" I was listening. Oh, yes, I was listening. I was listening to the way my heart pounded when he was this close to me. I was listening to the way my breathing came a little faster.

"Good luck," he said, then knocked on the door.

It opened, and a guy my age stood in front of us. He had blond hair like mine, a thin frame, and sharp features. If this was Maxwell, he looked nothing like the sexy dragon shifter I'd talked with at Thanksgiving in Emerald Pines.

A hardcover book lay face-down on the table just inside the door, the words *Advanced Alchemic Techniques* embossed on the front.

"Who's this?" the guy asked, staring a little too hard at me with his beady eyes.

"This is Morgan Rose," Vosovich said. "She's a late addition to the student body."

The guy looked me up and down. "Yeah, sure, okay."

I didn't think much of him, either.

"Where's Maxwell?" Vosovich asked.

"It's his night off."

So he wasn't Maxwell. That was good. This jerk would give Maxwells everywhere a bad name.

Vosovich looked less than pleased. "Well, I guess you'll need to find an empty bed for Morgan, help her get settled."

"Sure." The guy held out his hand. "I'm Devon, one of the hall assistants. Maxwell, the hall director, will be around tomorrow."

"Nice to meet you." I shook his hand and tried to ignore the clammy feeling of his palm against mine.

"Well, let's find you a room," Devon said, sitting down. He opened up a binder and ran a finger along the colored tabs at the side. Stopping at an orange one, he opened the pages. "Looks like you have two choices of roommates. Either Cora or Felicity."

I turned around to check on Vosovich, wondering if he had an opinion of those two students. He was already gone. I tried not to let it bother me—not that I needed his opinion, but he hadn't even said goodbye.

"It doesn't matter to me," I said to Devon. "Who do you recommend?"

He shrugged.

"All right, I'll go with Cora, then," I said.

He made a note on the page, then unlocked one of the desk drawers. He rummaged around it until he came up with an old key. "Here you go. Don't lose it."

I held it tight in my fist. This key represented my place here. I wouldn't go anywhere without it.

"Well, go on," he said. "It's room 2408."

He wasn't going to walk me there?

"I don't know where that is," I said.

"Go left, then go a ways. You'll find it."

I stared at him in disbelief. It seemed like he should help me out. But no, he was already leaning back in the desk chair and pulling his book into his lap.

"I take my studies seriously," he said when he noticed I hadn't gone away yet. "You should, too."

I left the room, feeling dazed. I didn't have books. I didn't have bedding. I'd left my clothes in my car. Hopefully Vosovich would bring them soon. All I had was a key and a stranger for a roommate.

The door to 2408 was closed when I reached it. I knocked and waited, but no one came to answer it.

"Hello?" I called. "It's Wre—Morgan, and I'm your new roommate."

Nothing happened. The crack at the bottom of the door was dark. I glanced down the hall, to several well-lit rooms, their doors open, their occupants laughing, talking, and listening to music. Likely, my roomie was out and about.

Suddenly, the door swung open, and a guy stood in front of me. He had tousled auburn hair that brushed the tops of his slate green eyes. He had an athletic build and a kind, handsome face. Obviously, he'd just pulled on a pair of jeans, because they weren't even buttoned. I tried not to stare at the trail of hair leading to his waistband.

I inhaled, trying to be subtle about it. This guy was a shifter, like me. Unlike me, he was some kind of big cat.

He stood maybe six inches taller than me, and from his height, he eyed me up and down. "I'm pretty sure you aren't my roommate."

I shook my head. "Not unless your name is Cora."

"Oh, that's my sister," he said. "What room are you looking for?"

"2408."

"She's in 2480. Come on, I'll take you there."

I walked next to him, wondering if I'd gotten the numbers wrong or if Devon had. I guessed it didn't really matter, as long as I ended up in the right place.

Looking over at the guy next to me, I said, "Sorry, did I wake you up?"

He nodded and ran a hand through his reddish brown hair. "Yeah, but it's no big deal. I'm Jace, by the way."

"You can call me Morgan." I had to be careful not to outright lie, because shifters could scent lies.

"Nice to meet you. So, why are you so late getting here?"

I shook my head. "Long story that I really don't want to get into."

"Where's your luggage?"

"Uh..."

"Part of the long story?" he said. "That's cool. But just so you know, secrets don't stay secret very long here at Spellbound."

Well, that was not ideal.

"Here," he said, taking my hand.

I stifled a gasp at the feeling of his skin on mine. His hand was warm and very lightly callused. The touch sent warmth up my arm and into my chest.

He looked down, his eyes wide. "Come here."

I didn't know this guy—at all—and yet I followed him around a corner to a very quiet, very dark corridor. I felt safe, but a niggling voice in the back of my head reminded me of my vision with the shadows and the bee.

"What are we doing?" I whispered.

Pulling a key from his jeans pocket, he opened a door, then stood back with a flourish.

"You need stuff," he said.

"Stuff?"

"Here you are."

I looked inside and found a storage closet. It was crammed full of junk.

"What is this?"

"One of the secrets at Spellbound that everyone knows about," he said. "You need something, chances are a student or five has left it here in the past. Look, there's even a trunk full of clothes, including some uniforms. You should see if it fits you. And some extra bedding—clean, I think."

"Wait, back up," I said. "Uniforms?"

"Yeah."

"Aren't we a little old for that?"

He shrugged. "More like *old fashioned*. Even though we're college-aged, this place was set up as a finishing school for witches, and the whole uniform thing kind of stuck."

"Okay." I wasn't going to complain. They were hiding me, and here I even had some free clothes and bedding.

Jace waited while I grabbed the trunk and a pile of sheets. The sheets still smelled like laundry detergent, so I was reassured.

When I came out of the closet, Jace took the trunk, his muscles bulging as he lifted it. I couldn't help staring, and when he caught my gaze, he winked.

Quickly, I looked away. "So, my room?"

"Just up here."

The door to 2480 was closed, like Jace's door had been, but unlike his room, this one had a light coming from beneath the door. Jace knocked the corner of the trunk against the door.

"Cora," he said, "I found you a friend."

I glanced up at him and grinned.

The door swung open and the girl behind it looked me up and down, much like her brother had done, but without the same heat in her gaze.

"Okay," she said, "you'll do."

"Cora," Jace said, "this is Morgan, your new roommate."

I looked at Jace, then back at Cora. "Hi, I hope you're okay with having a roommate."

"Yeppers," she said. "As long as you can be quiet while I study." She grabbed me by the wrist and yanked me into the room.

I looked around. There were two twin beds. One was obviously the bed Cora slept in, with a comforter and pillows and a plush unicorn. The other had a decorative throw on it and was covered in books.

"So, that's your bed," she said, pointing to the second one.

"Looks comfy," I said.

She laughed. "Hey, learning by osmosis could be a thing. Sleep on my books, get a better education than in old Tiddlywinks's class."

"Tiddlywinks?" I said. "Really?"

"Yep." She started moving books around, stacking them up next to one of the two desks.

"I'm sorry for making you rearrange stuff when you're already settled," I said.

"I don't mind, really," she said. "Jace, can you set the trunk over here at the foot of Morgan's bed?"

Jace brought in the trunk, set it down, and stood there awkwardly for a moment. "Can I get you anything else?"

A fluttery feeling came over my stomach. I wanted to spend more time with this guy. And it might have a little to do with how good he looked without a shirt on, but it had a lot to do with the way he smiled with half his mouth, like he was making fun of himself all the time. I liked that wry little smile.

But I was exhausted. I hadn't slept since two nights ago, and according to the schedule the chancellor had given me, I had a nine o'clock class in the morning. Theories of Prophecy.

"Go get your beauty rest, beast," Cora said to her brother.

He nodded. "Yeah. Nice to meet you, Morgan."

I wanted to tell him my real name and hear the way he said it, but instead I settled for, "It was nice to meet you, too."

He left the room, closing the door behind him, and Cora gave me a look.

"I can tolerate a lot of things," she said, "but if you have sex with my brother in this room, there will be a reckoning."

I laughed, but I felt myself blushing at the same time. "Got it."

There was an adjoining bathroom with just a toilet and sink. There must be communal showers somewhere else. I found a pair of pajamas in the trunk, so I got ready for bed, finger-brushing my teeth with some of Cora's toothpaste. Tomorrow I'd have to hunt down a toothbrush and toiletries of my own.

When I came out, there was a knock on the door. I rushed over to it, hoping to see Vosovich with the bag from my car. But when I opened the door, a girl I'd never seen before was holding my stuff. "Morgan Rose?" she asked.

"Yeah."

"Professor Vosovich asked me to deliver your things."

"Thanks," I said, trying to stifle the jealousy that she'd gotten to talk to him just now, and I hadn't.

The girl left and I turned to see Cora looking at me. Her eyes were a shade of gray green like her brother's, but slightly darker.

"Interesting," was all she said.

I decided not to comment on it.

Cora helped me make the bed. She gave me one of her pillows, and she even tossed me the plush unicorn.

"I don't know what your story is, Morgan, but you look like you could use a stuffie to cuddle with," she said. "Anyway, I'm glad you're here. Will the desk lamp bother you?"

"Nope," I said. "But thanks for asking."

She *tsked*. "So polite. They told you about the fifty percent cut-off for staying into year two, right?"

I nodded and snuggled into the blankets. The bed didn't smell like me yet; it still felt borrowed, not mine. But in time, I knew, I'd feel like I belonged.

"Well," Cora said, "make sure your politeness doesn't come back to bite you in the ass."

It was good advice—something Sparrow would have told me, actually. I thought of my sister, how she would fit in here, or rather, how she'd determinedly do everything in her power to *not* fit in. I didn't know what any of the rules were yet, but if Sparrow were here, she'd have already broken all of them.

Then again, it was me who'd crashed a car through their wards.

Maybe my days of following all the rules and being the nice Solaris sister were coming to an end.

CHAPTER 3

I had a uniform—a blue plaid skirt and a white, button-up blouse—and a pile of books. I was set-ish. Cora helped me find my first class, winding me through hallways and past other students. Girls wore either the blue plaid skirt like mine, or the black slacks and white button-up shirts with blue ties that the guys wore.

When I walked into the classroom, whatever confidence I'd mustered was completely gone. Theories of Prophecy, in theory, was the perfect fit for me.

There was a semi-circle of seats, with only one empty desk beside the only student I recognized, Devon, the not-so-friendly guy who'd told me the wrong room number. I took a seat, and found the teacher, a short woman with wild hair staring at me while she held a pale green paper in her hand. She wore something between a robe and a dress, of a whole rainbow of flowing fabrics. I offered a meek smile.

"Let's all welcome Ms. Rose to our class," she said in a deep voice that didn't match her rainbow dress. She dropped the paper onto her desk. "It's very unusual for a student to join after the start of the year, and completely unheard of for her to have no records."

I could feel everyone staring at me, but it was only Devon's pointed gaze that felt judgmental instead of curious.

"I expect you'll help Ms. Rose catch up on any information she's missed, right, Mr. Browning?"

"Of course." Devon nodded.

After the lecture started, Devon leaned over and whispered, "With you at the bottom, it's going to be all that much easier for me to reach the top fifty."

I ignored him and took notes. The lecture was all about the history of fortune telling. While interesting, given I'd never learned any of it before, none of it felt unmanageable either. I could study the important dates and events, and I'd learn it. I didn't just *want* to be here, I *needed* it. And I'd work my butt off to stay.

At the end of class, as students were packing up their things, I heard someone say my name—my fake name. "...one of the Guardians got Morgan. She forced her way in…"

How was I already getting a reputation for being disruptive?

"Yeah, but then she came *back*. Antoine heard Vosovich talking to the chancellor about it this morning before breakfast."

I left Prophecy class quickly, hoping to escape the buzz of rumors about me. Next, I had Conjuring and Calling Basics with Professor Arthur Burns. Apparently, it involved two parts—conjuring objects out of energy, and calling magical beings.

Professor Burns didn't introduce me as the newbie, which suited me just fine. Given the small class size, it wasn't like anyone wouldn't know anyway. And thankfully, no one was talking about how I'd gotten into the school.

Professor Burns jumped right in with asking everyone to

create a ball of light. The rows of students behind and in front of me did so right away, creating tiny balls of light in their palms. Devon, because apparently I was cursed to spend all day with this guy, looked back at me from the front row with a smug grin.

At least Jace was in here, too. He smiled at me from across the room.

"Light is the basis for all that we are as living beings." The professor walked up and down the rows, and then stopped beside a dark-haired girl. "Not so tight, Ms. Rodriguez."

I looked to the ball she held. It was shrinking to almost nothing, and then it flared out, a flash that took over the room.

Blinded for a moment, I felt my heart racing. When the light faded, Professor Burns was holding tight to the girl's wrist. The ball in her hand seemed to suck all the light from the room, making the overhead lights flicker.

He let go of her wrist, and it stabilized, a small glowing ball, just like everyone else's. No one else seemed phased.

The professor walked by my desk without stopping. I wasn't sure what I was supposed to be doing. If I should ask how exactly to create a ball, or… But I wasn't going to get anything out of this if I didn't ask. So I raised my hand.

He ignored me. "It's not a ball in the sky, or a bulb hanging from the ceiling. It's a flow, a net of strings that connects all of us."

Using my witch's sight like I had with the ward, I looked up at the lights above me and I saw it, I saw the magic. I reached up, drawn to the vibrant glow, and instinctively, I plucked one of the strings. My hand was enveloped in a soft glow of white light, and my breath caught.

Everyone turned to stare, but all I could focus on was my hand and the light surrounding it like a glove. I turned my palm and the light shimmered. I pinched, lifting it from a glove to a mountain in my palm.

"Very good, Ms. Rose." The professor nodded to me.

At the end of class, when we put the lights out, the world felt a little darker, a little colder than it had been.

"Do you feel that?" Jace asked, bumping my shoulder as we followed the line of students out of the room.

"The dullness?"

"Yeah. It's strange, right?" He smiled, and an adorable dimple formed on his cheek.

I nodded.

"You were amazing in there. Tell me, have you created light before?"

"No." I looked at my hand, remembering the feel of it. "And I don't think I made it."

"You wove it."

"Yeah."

He nodded. "You're going to do just fine here."

"Thanks."

"What do you have next?"

"Philosophy of Magic," I said.

He cringed. It was faint, held back, but I caught it. "That bad?"

"No. It's not bad." I could hear the lie in his words. He was a shifter, so he'd know I could. "Okay, it's not a first choice. But you'll do great. Want me to walk you there?"

"That'd be nice, thank you."

After a few minutes of walking, we stopped in front of a spiral stone stairwell.

"This is it." Jace gestured to the stairwell, which was quiet and dark. I heard laughter coming from out of sight, but it echoed strangely against the stone.

"Not foreboding at all," I said.

He laughed, and I couldn't help but smile. "Good luck."

"Why exactly do I need luck?" I asked as he started to walk away.

He turned around, walking backward as he looked at me. "Don't volunteer for any debates, and you'll be fine."

"Got it, thanks." I waved and watched him go. He wore that uniform well, the black pants tailored to his nice butt.

Downstairs, there was a big chalkboard, and the seats were split down the middle, two groups facing each other, as if in opposition. I hoped avoiding debates would be as easy as Jace had suggested. I was happy to hang back and learn, completely content with not volunteering. I took a seat as everyone else was filing in, and lucky me, straight across from me was Devon.

Once all the seats were filled, everyone stopped talking. In the silence, I could hear footsteps coming down the stairs. I watched the doorway, wondering what Professor Belinda Juarez would be like.

But the person who stepped through the door was definitely *not* Professor Juarez.

Walking in like he owned the place was none other than Maxwell Phillips. He was a gorgeous dragon shifter with a tall, lean build, impossibly blue eyes beneath bangs of dirty-blond hair, and a grumpy disposition. He was a part of my past, the last person I'd expected to see here, someone I never expected to see again. Instantly I felt the same heat cross my skin that I had at Thanksgiving. I'd been in a bad place emotionally, hiding out in Emerald Pines after being held prisoner in a cell for so long.

There was a connection between us, one I was happy to deny. The connection told me that this man was meant to be mine. Like I needed more problems.

His eyes were glued to me as he entered. What was he doing here?

He flipped through the book in his hand, to a green paper

that was tucked inside. I'd seen the pale green paper in my other two classes. The professors had looked at it before either finding me or announcing me. Why did Maxwell have it?

He tilted his chin slightly to the side and his eyes sparkled with questions as he looked to me. Then he turned his attention to the class and stood in the center of the room, in the divide between the two sides.

Maxwell was my teacher.

The other teachers had known I was coming, they'd known they were getting a new student named *Morgan.* But Maxwell knew my real name. He knew me as Wren Solaris, the broken oracle. Would he call me out on it?

"Today we'll be discussing the morality and consequences of deceptive magic." He scanned one side of the room and then the other, this time looking everywhere but at me. "Let us first list the *acceptable* types."

The look Maxwell shot the guy in the corner suggested that not all deceptive magic was acceptable, and that guy was likely to point out the others. I didn't even know there *was* deceptive magic, or what it did beyond the obvious—deceiving people.

"Memory manipulation," a voice said from somewhere behind me.

Maxwell nodded and straightened his blue tie. "Very good. When used responsibly, memory manipulation is permitted. What else?"

Images of the monster in the woods filled my head. It had caught me before, and I hadn't even remembered that when it tried to grab me again. People were still talking, but I found myself trapped in wondering what memories I'd lost.

"Appearance distortion," someone else answered.

"Very good." Maxwell moved toward the end of the room. "That's enough to get us started. Who would like to lead?"

Devon raised his hand.

"Very well, Mr. Browning." Maxwell gestured to Devon before stepping back.

Devon puffed out his chest and rose to his feet. His arrogant grin suggested he loved the spotlight. Good for him. He could have it.

"Memory magic...remembering to stay in your place." He shot me a look. Ugh.

Or forgetting your manners. I held my lips tight and kept that to myself.

"How does it feel to have your memories taken away, Morgan?" A nasty smile played on Devon's lips.

My cheeks heated with everyone looking at me. I shrugged it off. "I don't remember."

A few people laughed, including the girl beside me. Then she leaned over. "What's it like to be grabbed by one of the Guardians? Did it hurt? They got you twice, didn't they? That's what I heard."

"Let's steer back on track," Maxwell walked down the aisle. "How about the morality of using the Guardians?"

"It's important to have protection for the school," someone said.

"But where do you draw the line with taking people's memories?" someone else asked. "Like what if you screwed up a first impression on a date? Would it be okay to, say, pretend it didn't happen?"

Conversation bounced around the room.

"Wouldn't that be nice?"

"I did that once."

"But how many times can you do that before it's really messed up?"

"One time is mean enough."

It went on like that for what felt like an eternity. And I tried to just keep my head down, trying not to be the focus of conversation. It went mostly okay, until it was time to leave.

As I was packing up, Maxwell spread his hands on my desk. I held my breath, caught in his fiery blue gaze. It was just like Thanksgiving, with those mesmerizing eyes on mine. I'd thrown myself at him, desperate to feel his skin. We'd talked for hours, and I'd thought he felt the same. So I'd climbed into his lap and tried to kiss him.

But he'd gripped my wrists, drawing them away from his shoulders, and walked away.

And then I'd run.

All I wanted was for him to turn away now, to pretend we didn't know each other. But no way that was going to happen. He was going to tell me to stay after class. This whole thing was going to get weirder. I wanted out. Out of this room, out of this class.

"Welcome to Spellbound Academy." Maxwell stood up and gave me a knowing grin. It was hot and teasing and tempting all at the same time. "Best of luck, *Morgan.*"

I let out the breath I was holding, and rushed out of there as quickly as I could.

At the top of the stairs, I saw Cora walking down the hall. I raced to catch up with her. "Cora!"

She stopped and turned. "Hey. Was that your last class?"

"Thankfully, yes."

"How was it?"

I was exhausted. "Amazing and terrifying and overwhelming."

"Welcome to Spellbound." When she said it, her words were melodic and genuine. She giggled, which made me laugh. "Ready to start studying?"

"Yes. No." Maybe there was a way to switch classes. It could be magical toilet cleaning at three in the morning for all I cared, I just had to get away from Maxwell. "There's something I need to do first. If I can. Do you think there's any way I can get out of Philosophy of Magic? Or maybe just take it with a different professor?"

"I seriously doubt it. There's never any changing classes, no drops, no adds. Well, except for them letting you in here late. And the TA isn't *that* bad, is he?"

"Maxwell Phillips is the TA?" That made more sense than him being a professor, because I'd thought he was closer to my age.

"Yeah," she said, "he's a second-year, like me. Why? He's standoffish, but he isn't mean or anything."

I frowned and shook my head. "Is there a class on eating glass? I'll take that one. Anything so long as it's away from Maxwell Phillips."

The color drained from Cora's face and she waved her hand like I needed to stop talking. I turned slowly, knowing but hoping I was wrong.

Standing there looking at me, most definitely in earshot, was Maxwell Phillips.

CHAPTER 4

The rest of the week went much like the first day. Classes Monday, Wednesday, and Friday. Tuesday and Thursday were spent studying like a crazy person while I tried to catch up. It wasn't just the first part of the semester I'd missed, but a lifetime of magic infused into life. Most of the other students had spent their childhoods training to come here, which meant I was more than a few pages behind everyone else.

After that first day in Philosophy of Magic, Maxwell didn't treat me any differently from the other students. Besides being overwhelmed with the course load, I was very quickly falling into a routine. My favorite parts of the week were Conjuring and Calling, walking with Jace, and studying with Cora. Because she was a year ahead, she knew all the answers to all of my questions, and she was fun to hang out with.

And before I knew it, it was Friday and my first week was almost over.

Lunch on Friday could only be described as loud. Several round tables were set up in the large dining hall, and they seemed more packed than usual, although the room still held the same number of students and staff. The energy of the place was crackling, electric. It was a little too much, and the September day was warm, so I took my smoothie and sandwich out to the courtyard and found a bench in the sun.

Cora slid onto the bench beside me so hard, I nearly spilled my smoothie.

"Too bad it's forbidden to hook up with teachers," she said.

"What?" I laughed.

She gestured across the courtyard to a man in a well-tailored suit. He had sharp features and wild hair.

"Professor O'Leary," Cora said. "I wouldn't mind breaking a few rules for him."

"You?" With as hard as Cora worked, I had a hard time imagining her as a rule breaker.

"Oh, I know how to have fun," she said. "You're coming tonight, right?"

"Another study session?" I said, inwardly groaning. The girl was a machine. I'd never met anyone as smart or dedicated as her.

"No. All work and no play leads to burn-out," she said. "There's a party tonight, and you're coming."

"Oh, I don't know..."

"Oh, yes you do," she said. "It'll be fun, and you need to give your brain a break. You've been studying nearly as much as I have, and that's not healthy."

I laughed and swiped one of her french fries. "Fine. As long as you're there."

"Well, *someone* needs to help me keep Cora in line," a deep voice said from behind us.

I looked up to see Jace leaning against the back of the bench.

"She can't do that herself?" I asked him.

Cora stuck her tongue out at her brother and said, "Have a seat. If you're going to make fun of me, at least join us for lunch."

There was more space next to her than next to me, so I was surprised when he squeezed himself in between me and the arm of the bench. His body was hard against mine, and if his sister hadn't been right next to me, I'd have been tempted to scoot even closer to him.

We talked and ate our lunches, but pretty soon, Jace was looking at his watch.

"Only two more classes today," Jace said, "and then we get to show you the real Spellbound Academy."

* * *

IN THE DARKNESS of the courtyard, Cora nudged me past the gates toward the outer grounds.

"Are you *sure* it's safe?" I asked.

I hadn't realized the party would be out in the woods—I'd figured we would all meet in someone's room, or maybe the dormitory common room.

"Of course it's safe," she said.

"Have you *seen* those Guardians?" My voice was higher-pitched than I would've wanted it. Suddenly, I wished Vosovich were out here with us.

But he was a teacher and part of the school's security team. I was pretty sure he wouldn't be invited to this kind of revelry. Which meant buzzkill Maxwell wouldn't be, either. That right there was a good reason for me to get out and have some fun.

I missed Sparrow something fierce. Cora was a lot like her. Sparrow would also make it her mission to get me to a party. Probably after spiking my soda at dinner.

"The Guardians only go after people trying to break in,"

Cora said. "They're not going after students who actually belong here."

But did they know I belonged here now? Or did they hold a grudge?

"Come on." Cora linked her arm in mine and passed me a flask.

I didn't care what was in it; I obviously needed some liquid courage, so I uncapped the flask and poured a big swallow down my throat. It burned, and I coughed.

Cora rubbed my back and we giggled together. This would be fine—there wouldn't be two dozen students wandering around the woods if it was really dangerous. And already my limbs were feeling lighter and warmer, an effect of the alcohol.

A faint orange light glowed beyond the trees, surrounded by moving shadows. The movement wasn't just shadows, but little creatures, no bigger than bowling balls, with fluffy blue fur and the long ears of rabbits. Except *they were flying.*

The crackling of a fire reached my ears. Guitar music rose up to the sky, or maybe it was a ukulele—it sounded higher-pitched than a guitar. People laughed and talked. The noise was like the dorms after classes were out, with students relaxing and hanging out together.

Beyond the trees, the little flying bunnies spun and flipped through the air, enjoying a celebration of their own in the shadows of the flickering firelight.

Studying would be smarter. Coming out here was not the best use of my time. There was still so much catching up to do.

As we got closer to the light, a couple of guys rushed forward.

"Cora!" one of them said, and kissed her full on the mouth, right in front of me.

Then the other one did the same thing.

I stared.

Cora laughed. "Morgan, these are my boyfriends, Blake and Thomas."

"Boyfriends?" I said. She hadn't said anything about one boyfriend, much less two.

"She ignores us all week to study, but the weekends belong to us," the guy on the left said. He held out his hand. "I'm Blake."

I shook his hand, and then Thomas's, and the guys offered to get us drinks.

"Yes, please," I said.

"Yes, please," Cora mimicked me in a prissy voice, but wrapped her arm around my shoulders so I didn't feel stupid. "You're still so polite."

We got closer to the fire, and I saw it wasn't a typical bonfire, but a collection of magical light spheres like what we'd created in Conjuring and Calling. Most of them were yellow and orange, but there were some different colors thrown into the mix—blue, green, purple, pink. I stared at the lights, unable to tear my gaze away.

The daily grind version of Spellbound Academy was grueling study and cutthroat student jockeying. Yet this time in the woods was more about magic and whimsy. Of the two versions of Spellbound Academy I'd encountered, this one was better already.

One of the bunnies landed on a tree branch by the edge of the clearing. It had a torn ear and a patch of white fur between its eyes. And it seemed to be staring at me, with its tiny wings beating like a hummingbird's from its back.

"Lapinfées," Cora said.

I looked to her.

"They're drawn to drinking and noise. They always come when we have a bonfire."

"They're adorable."

She nodded. "Come on."

"Morgan, you came," a deep voice said next to me.

I pulled my focus from the fire to look up at Jace. "Hey."

"Hey." He knocked my shoulder with his, then held up a flask. "Want some?"

"Sure, thanks." I took a swig. It burned going down, but not as badly as Cora's had, and this time I didn't cough. Sparrow would be so proud of me, I thought with a wry grin.

People had dragged over fallen logs to sit on, and some had even brought lawn chairs with them, which they perched on while they talked and drank. Most people stood, though. A student from my Theories of Prophecy class was playing the ukulele, strumming along and singing quietly with a couple of other guys and girls.

"So, are you glad you came?" Jace asked.

I moved closer to him so I could feel the heat of his arm through my sweater. "Definitely."

The ukulele music stopped, and someone said, "We need a game!"

"A kissing game," someone else shouted.

"Annnnd, that's my cue to leave," I murmured to Jace.

He laughed. "Stick around. You can just watch if you want."

Reassured, I watched as a few people got into a circle. I'd been expecting something like spin the bottle, so I was surprised when one of them conjured a little glowing ball of light and moved her hand up and down so it bounced in the air. With each bounce, it changed color.

Cora was in the circle and saw me watching. "Get in here, Morgan!"

I shook my head. "Nope."

"Your loss," she said.

The girl with the ball of light tossed it across the circle to another girl, who caught it and then threw it to a guy. With each catch, the ball changed color. Orange, blue, purple, green. Lapinfée jumped around hysterically, as if waiting for something big to happen. But nobody was kissing.

"How does this game work?" I asked Jace.

"If it turns red, the person who threw it and the person who catches it have to kiss."

"Oh," I said, just as Cora threw the ball to Thomas. It turned red.

Everyone cheered as Cora and Thomas walked over to each other and kissed. It was no chaste, two-second kiss, either. I was doubly glad for not joining the game.

"Not everyone has to kiss like that," Jace said, laughing.

On the next throw, the ball turned red again, and two girls gave each other a delicate kiss on the lips. Everyone cheered again.

Suddenly, the ball came out of the circle, right toward me. Jace snatched it out of the air and laughed. "We're lucky it didn't turn red, Mikhail."

The guy who'd thrown it, Mikhail, laughed. "I'd kiss you, Jace."

Jace tossed the ball back into the circle, where a girl with curly brown hair caught it. The ball turned red.

"He's not even playing," she said, pouting. "Ouch!"

"What's wrong?" I asked, as Jace trotted away from me, over to the girl.

Another girl near me said, "The ball will burn the palms of the people who threw and caught it unless they kiss."

"Harsh," I said, watching with a spike of jealousy in my gut as Jace pecked the girl on the lips.

The girl near me shrugged. "That's the game. It's no fun if people don't follow the rules."

I stayed put, not wanting to get anywhere close to the circle.

"What's going on out here?" a low voice called.

Oh shit. I recognized that voice. My suspicions were confirmed when people started chanting, "Max-well, Max-well."

When I closed my eyes I remembered the feel of his skin against my neck, the deep fiery cinnamon of his scent, the hot cider on his breath that I could almost taste. But he'd pushed me away.

Another girl was currently holding the ball of light, which glowed green. She tossed it toward Maxwell. "Hey, Maxwell, catch!"

He caught the ball of light, which turned blue in his hands. Staring at it for a second, he shook his head. "No, I'm not playing."

"You have to throw it," someone said.

Shaking his head, he pulled back his arm to throw the ball. At that moment, a couple of giggling drunk guys stumbled into him.

I didn't know where he'd intended the ball to go—maybe straight up to the moon, or maybe to someone in particular in the circle. But instead, it flew directly at me.

There was no time to think. Instinctively, I reached out and caught the ball.

It turned red.

Everyone cheered.

There had to be rules against TAs and students kissing, right? I shook my head slightly, and hazarded a glance at Maxwell.

He looked absolutely revolted.

Well, that stung more than a little.

I didn't know how to get rid of the ball. If I threw it really fast, maybe the magic would move on.

My palm started to itch. In the glowing red light of the ball, it looked redder than it should have. The itch turned into heat, and a burn. I was determined to suck it up. I'd let my whole freaking hand fall off before I kissed some asshole who was so obviously repulsed by me.

"Kiss, kiss, kiss!" everyone chanted.

Jace was staring at me, his eyes wide. "That has to hurt," he called.

It did. It hurt like a motherfucker. My eyes were watering, but I blinked back the tears. Fire was nothing to my pride.

Cora came over and tried to drag me toward Maxwell.

"No," I said.

"Stop being stubborn," she said.

I planted my feet on the ground, grinding my teeth against the burning feeling of my skin. I wanted to wail at the heat, but I refused to let a single sound come out. My only comfort was that Maxwell had to be feeling the same agony.

The lapinfées made clicking sounds from between the trees, as if cheering or goading us on.

Suddenly, Maxwell was standing right in front of me.

"Morgan," he said, his voice mocking. "Look up."

Damn him, he wasn't giving any sign that he was hurt.

I shook my head.

"Come on," he said, "I'm not that ugly."

No, but I obviously was, from the look he'd given me a few moments ago. From the way he'd pushed me off him at Thanksgiving.

He tilted my chin up with his finger. The burning feeling in my hand lessened. I'd met a few dragons before, and they all carried a scent that I could only describe as "burnt sky." Maxwell's, though, was unique to me; I'd recognize him anywhere. As I breathed him in, the memory of our night on the roof was as clear as if it had just happened.

"I need your consent, Morgan," he whispered.

Cora spoke up. "That's it, I'm calling the game. Someone make this stop, whoever conjured it."

"Hang on," a girl said, then started muttering under her breath, undoing the spell.

The pain lessened until it was gone. Maxwell still stood in front of me, his hand cupping my chin. I had to look up into his intense blue eyes. The expression in them was turbulent —dislike, desire.

"Do I have your consent?" he asked.

He was still pushing this, even when the magic was ending?

He didn't like me, yet I could tell he wasn't repulsed by me. He *wanted* me. Infuriating man. Maybe giving me a bland peck on the lips was just the punishment he deserved.

Feeling pissy and contrary, I said, "Yes, you have my consent."

The kiss was not bland like I'd expected—far from it. It was bruising and punishing—there was nothing sweet or soft as his lips met mine. They moved against me in a way that made me sigh into him. Taking advantage of my parted lips, he swiped his tongue against them. I opened more, and gripped his arms as if holding him in place. He tasted like cinnamon, fiery sweet.

Someone wolf-whistled, and I pulled back from Maxwell, shocked.

His gaze met mine, both surprised and full of lust. Then he turned on his heel and marched back to the school.

I stood frozen in place, watching his retreat until Jace came up to my side.

"Wow," he said.

I looked up at him. "Wow, what?"

He leaned down and whispered in my ear, too faint for anyone else to hear him, "That was a fucking turn-on."

CHAPTER 5

The world was swirly and warm and confusing. Maybe that was just my stomach, and maybe my head, too. That wasn't the kind of kiss that was given to someone you hated. It was the kind of kiss that was packed full of promises. Promises of what, I had no idea. Of calling on me in class when I didn't know anything about the subject matter? Maybe. Of anger at me that I'd left Emerald Pines without a word to him about where I was going or what I was doing? It wasn't like I had known at the time, anyway. Besides, Maxwell and I didn't have a relationship. We didn't know each other, not really. We'd shared a couple of hours under the stars, talking. Just talking. I didn't owe Maxwell anything. I hadn't owed him the kiss, but I didn't regret it either.

I just couldn't stop thinking about it.

Everyone was heading out, as morning light twinkled on the horizon, bits of sun breaking through the trees. I stared at the flames that weren't flames from my place on a log.

Cora stepped between me and the glow. "You okay?"

"Yeah, I'm fine."

"Everyone's going in. You ready?"

I glanced over to the two guys waiting for Cora. It was sweet that she wanted to be there for me, but if I had two boyfriends who looked like hers, I didn't know that I'd ever be able to tear myself away from them. Or at least that's what I'd want to do, in theory. It was what Sparrow would do, and I'd always wished I was more like my sister—unafraid, free. And like Sparrow, Cora deserved to have fun.

"You can go," I said. "I'm fine."

She narrowed her eyes at me.

"I'm not quite ready to go yet, either." Jace sat down on the log beside me. "We're good. You go ahead."

Cora smiled. "All right. Have fun, you two."

"Do everything I wouldn't do," I said, smiling at her.

She laughed and joined her boyfriends.

I leaned into Jace's shoulder. With the way he was looking at me, I wondered if he was still thinking about that kiss, too. *That was a fucking turn-on.* A rush of heat washed over me thinking about his words. What if I could have the same thing Cora had? What if I could have Jace *and* Maxwell? If I was indulging in fantasy, why not throw in that hot angry wolf who'd rescued me—Vosovich. If I had the nerve, I'd happily take all three.

But I didn't. I couldn't.

Maybe Cora had the right idea. I didn't need to be polite, or cling to any of the other traits that had landed me a prisoner. *Wren* wouldn't break the rules or even consider the idea of being with more than one guy. But at Spellbound, I wasn't Wren. I was Morgan.

Emboldened by my new sense of self, I laced my fingers in Jace's. He turned to me, and the rainbow of unearthly firelight twinkled in his eyes. Excitement skittered up my spine. He didn't know who I'd been before—none of the students did. I could be whoever I wanted to be, do whatever I wanted to do.

My attention lowered to his lips, to the playful smile that he always seemed to put on. Maybe he wasn't keeping a secret joke that was just for him; maybe that grin was for me.

What I wanted to do was kiss him, so I did.

His lips were soft and gentle. He was everything Maxwell wasn't. And this kiss was everything the last one wasn't. Jace tasted like bourbon and contentment, like a mashup of thrill and comfort. And I liked it.

A shiver carried across my skin, like an icy gale in the summer heat. Something was wrong. I pulled away.

"That was—" Jace smiled at me.

But behind him, I caught a flash of movement in the trees. I looked up in time to see a giant trunk crashing down toward us. I jumped to my feet, and before I could say a word, Jace tackled me to the ground.

The tree crashed down beside us, burying the fire, crushing the log where we had just been. An inhuman howl echoed through the forest, and a Guardian stepped out from between the trees. I scrambled to get out from under Jace, but he wouldn't move.

"Get up. We have to...Jace?"

His leg was caught.

"I'm stuck." He pulled and twisted, but his leg was pinned.

I wiggled out from under him, grabbed his wrist and pulled. He wouldn't budge.

"Run, Morgan."

"I won't leave you." Panic welled in my chest as the monster approached, giant footsteps resonating through the forest floor. "Come on. I can get you out of this."

I grabbed him, wrapping my arms around his chest, but he still wouldn't budge. The tree was too big to lift, and I was running out of time.

The monster swung its big arm toward me. I dove to the ground, the wake of the swipe pulling the air with it. The monster's single eye was locked on me. Maybe it hadn't forgiven that I'd broken in here. Maybe it knew I didn't belong.

I hopped up to my feet and ran a couple of yards away. The monster's gaze followed. It reached for me, and I ducked behind a tree. It wasn't interested in Jace. I had to lead it away. I had to...I didn't even know.

The air began to move in a strange way, pushed down with oppressive force. I looked up to the half-dark sky and saw a blue creature with massive wings. A dragon. Its bright blue eyes surveyed the forest.

This wasn't just any dragon; this was *Maxwell.*

He circled above us once, twice, then lowered his body down, tucking in his wings and crowding the clearing where the fire had been. Then he put his claw on the tree that had been crushing Jace. Panic thrummed in my veins, but Jace wasn't there. Only his clothes were left on the ground. He must have shifted.

I turned around, searching for him. In front of me stood a huge cat with tan fur—a mountain lion. I knew by scent that this was Jace. He'd shifted to escape the tree. Good thinking.

The Guardian charged toward us. I ran, swerving between trees, knowing the monster was closing in.

Maxwell was here. Jace was here. Still, I found myself wishing I had Vosovich here too, with his glowing rope. Rope—that was it!

I hid behind a tree, and the forest grew quiet. I peeked around the corner. The monster was standing still only a few feet away. It lifted its nose to the air.

I tried to dislodge one of the vines dangling down from the treetops, to no avail.

Jace bumped my thigh with his lion nose, and in his

mouth was one of the vines I was trying to grab. It was like he'd read my mind.

I smiled down at him. "Thank you."

The monster must have heard me, because the sound of its footsteps were closing in.

I took one end of the vine and Jace took the other. When the Guardian reached us, we circled around, pulling the vine around its legs. I came back around, and Jace shifted back to human form. Under any other circumstances, I'd definitely take the time to appreciate every inch of his sculpted naked form.

The monster turned and struggled against the bindings, keeping its attention locked on me. It swung its fist down toward my head. I jumped out of the way just in time.

"Throw me your end," Jace said.

As soon as I did, he tightened and tied off the vine. The monster didn't fall like it had when Vosovich had tied it up. Instead, it flexed its legs, testing its footing.

Jace backed up and ran back over to me.

"It won't hold," I said.

"We should run."

I nodded and turned, racing back the way we had come, toward the clearing, toward the school, toward safety. The sound of the vine snapping was like the revving of a chainsaw in a horror movie.

When we reached the clearing, I'd expected Maxwell to still be there. He wasn't. I looked up and found him in the sky above, raining fire in a large circle around us. Trapping us. *Why?*

He descended, diving between the trees, and when he rose again, the Guardian was twisting in his claws. He threw the creature, tossing it outside the circle before lowering back down to the clearing.

Enveloped in a soft glow, the dragon returned to the

shape of a man. A naked man, with a lean yet muscular frame.

"What the hell, Maxwell?" I put my hands on my hips, expecting some kind of explanation. Instead, he only spared me a glance before heading toward the trees and brush nearby.

I followed after him.

The fire roared, an unmoving wall that he seemed to be heading straight for.

"Why are you—" I grabbed his arm, but he pulled away and dove at someone who seemed to be hiding behind a tree.

Maxwell tackled the dude to the ground, and then I saw who it was—Devon the Prick.

Devon flinched as Maxwell jabbed him in the nose. Devon cupped his face with both hands. While part of me wanted to defend an innocent person, the other part wasn't exactly disappointed to see him get hit.

"What was that for?" Devon's words were garbled as he held his face. The faint scent of blood tinged the air.

"You know." Maxwell growled and climbed off of him.

"I don't." I shifted my weight to get into Maxwell's line of sight.

"He drew the Guardian to you."

"How would he do that?" Jace stepped up beside me, gloriously naked, which was a distraction. But it was a good question.

"That's crazy. You're crazy." Devon scrambled away until his back hit the trunk of the tree he'd been hiding behind.

"Deception spell." Maxwell kicked a book on the ground that I hadn't noticed before. My guess—a spell book. "I saw him weave the magic onto the Guardian. What I don't know is why."

"You were trying to hurt her?" Jace stepped between me and Devon, and he closed his hands into fists, like he too wanted to take a swing at the guy. If anyone was going to do that, it should be me.

"Dude, put some clothes on. It wasn't supposed to hurt anyone." Devon rose to his feet and held his head high. There was blood running down over his lips and his nose was swollen.

I cringed at the sight. Yeah, he'd probably had enough.

"You expected it to steal her memories?" Maxwell asked. "Casting magic on a Guardian is a serious offense."

"I only wanted to scare her."

"Why?" I asked, stepping between Maxwell and Jace. "Why would you want to scare me? I haven't done anything to you."

"You show up out of nowhere, thinking you're better than everyone else. You don't belong here."

"That's enough." Maxwell waved a hand, and the fire disappeared. "Straight to Vosovich with you."

Devon ran.

"How serious an offense is it?" I asked.

"His mommy is rich," Maxwell sneered. "He'll get a slap on the wrist, nothing more. Entitled asshole. I'd never depend on my family's money to get out of trouble."

"And why Vosovich? Why not the chancellor?" I pressed. This seemed serious enough for her.

"V takes care of stuff in the evenings. He'll only bother her if there's a life-threatening issue. Since everyone is okay, he'll make a report to her in the morning." Maxwell ran a hand through his dirty-blond hair and frowned. "He still won't get the punishment he deserves. I'm glad I punched him in the nose."

I gave him a grim smile. "Me, too."

CHAPTER 6

Jace found his pants on the ground and pulled them on. I looked away, giving him some privacy, but if I found his shirt anywhere, I'd kick it behind a bush. A guy like him should be shirtless as much as possible.

Maxwell remained nearby, glaring at me, not even bothering to cover his junk. Then again, he didn't have anything he should hide, either—he was well-endowed.

A flash of white t-shirt caught my eye, next to the crushed log. With my foot, I carefully shoved it behind the nearest tree trunk. Jace wouldn't miss the plain shirt, and as far as I was concerned, I was doing the universe a favor.

"You okay?" Jace asked, coming back to my side.

I looked up guiltily, then nodded. Everything came back in a rush. The attack, the running. Adrenaline had stopped pumping through me, and in its wake was exhaustion.

I opened my mouth to speak, and then felt tears forming in my eyes. Angrily, I blinked them away. Tears were not warranted here. Sparrow wouldn't cry. She'd be pissed. Pissed, like I was.

"Hey," Jace said, tugging me into a half hug.

Maxwell looked like he would come over, too, but he frowned at us and cocked his head. What was he thinking? I wondered if Spellbound Academy had a class on mind reading, because I could really use that skill when it came to Maxwell.

Then again, as he frowned harder and shifted back into his dragon, I worried about what I'd find in that head of his. Nothing flattering about me, that was for sure.

"Come on," Jace said, pulling away slightly so he could hold my hand, "let's report to V."

"Are you friends with him or something?" I asked. "You've been calling him V."

He shrugged. "It's shorter than Vosovich, and he's never told me not to."

As we walked through the quiet forest, I found it difficult not to stare at Jace. Kicking his shirt behind that tree was definitely a good call. The taste of his kiss still lingered on my lips and even though we were going to deal with what Devon had done, all I could think about was the sweet and gorgeous man beside me.

"You don't have to tell me." His playful eyes flickered in the moonlight. "Did you really break through the wards with no training?"

I'd been bothered when everyone else had talked about me, but I didn't mind Jace asking. He could ask me anything...except my name. A pang of regret filled my chest.

"I did."

"Did you learn about wards from your parents?"

"No. I just knew how to do it," I said, holding tightly to his hand. He felt good connected to me. "I didn't learn much magic at all from my mom. My dad's side is all shifters. How about you?"

Up ahead, there was a small stone building at the edge of

the clearing by the academy. It was up against a small courtyard, which was lined with ivy-covered walls and...were those gargoyles? As we got closer, I realized that yes, they were. I was torn between feeling impressed at the massive statues, and disappointed at the cliché of their existence.

Jace continued, "My whole pack is a mix of shifters and witches. Like most of the students here, my family has been coming to Spellbound for generations to learn and to get a chance at working for one of the big corporations."

"That's what this academy is for?" I asked. "Finding jobs?"

He shrugged. "More or less. Second years are after fancy jobs. That's why they don't have the same restriction as us first years, where only half of them can succeed. But their exams are hard, and only about half do. Of those who do well, only a few get recruited."

"And you said something about corporations?"

"There are two in the States. MagiCorp and Geard Enterprises. Being chosen is a huge honor, and sets you up for life. All the money you could dream of, and then some."

"Wow."

"No one in my family's ever been chosen," he said, "and Cora's determined to be the first."

"What about you?"

"I haven't decided what I want to do yet." Jace stopped walking in front of the little stone building. "We're here."

Jace knocked on the door with the hand that wasn't holding mine.

"Come in," Vosovich said.

Jace and I walked inside, still holding hands. I didn't want to let him go. Something about touching him felt right—right like I'd felt when I kissed Maxwell, right like I'd felt when kissing Jace a moment ago, and the same way I felt when being around Vosovich.

His office was dim, with windows all around letting in

the moonlight. A single, old-fashioned lamp sat on the desk, and nothing else. Behind the desk was a swivel chair, and in front of it were two plain folding chairs.

Devon was already here, a trickle of blood beneath his nose from where Maxwell had punched him. I avoided looking at him, still too full of rage to trust myself. It wasn't just me that the Guardian could have hurt—it could've hurt anyone else out there tonight. Even stupid Devon.

"Mr. Browning told me what he did," Vosovich said, his dark gaze hard and angry as he looked at Devon.

I nodded. Devon wouldn't have been able to lie to Vosovich, a shapeshifter.

"While his punishment is not your business," Vosovich continued, "you should know he is being dealt with accordingly, and his parents will be apprised of the situation."

I nodded again, feeling kind of unnecessary. Why was I here?

Vosovich kept his gaze on Devon. "I'll see you here at oh-five-hundred on Monday."

Looking completely cowed, Devon slinked out of the office. But when he walked past me, he bumped me hard with his shoulder.

"Asshole," Jace coughed.

I agreed.

Jace and I turned back to Vosovich. Something in Vosovich's gaze made Jace drop my hand, and I shot him a questioning glance.

"Mr. Gladstone, you can go," Vosovich said.

I looked from one to the other. Vosovich still hadn't acknowledged me—did he even care that I was here?

Jace turned to leave, so I turned alongside him.

"Ms. Rose, remain behind."

The growling order in his voice halted me in my tracks.

Jace turned around and gave me a little smile before disappearing into the courtyard.

Slowly, I spun to face Vosovich. The short stubble on his cheeks was distracting. I wanted to touch them, feel them against my face as I kissed him. He wore his usual black pants and shirt, and his short, dark hair reminded me of the military. I wondered if he had served in the military.

"You have a knack for getting into trouble," he said.

"This was all Devon," I said, trying not to sound like a pouting child. "I had nothing to do with bringing over that Guardian."

"True," he said, "but that doesn't change what I said. Trouble keeps coming for you."

I remained still as he approached, stalking toward me like the wolf he was, looking just like the trouble he was telling me about. A huge gray wolf, creeping ever closer, waiting to pounce on its prey—me.

I wasn't only prey to him, either. I could see the way his gaze darkened, the way he moved carefully, the way his pants stretched over his hardening cock.

He wanted me. Desired me. But from the way he made his hands into fists, he was fighting it.

I thought about the fantasy I'd enjoyed before the Guardian had attacked, about taking whoever I wanted, and screw the consequences. Screw being nice.

Wren would never go up to a teacher. She would never put her hand on him. Never flutter her eyelashes and slowly, deliberately bite her lip before letting it go.

But Morgan? She would do those things.

I stepped closer. I placed my palm against his chest, just above his heart. I batted my eyelashes and bit my lip as I stared at his mouth.

Vosovich's breath caught in his throat. His pupils dilated

even more, no doubt at the scent of my desire in the air. We were shifters—we couldn't hide those things from each other.

"So, what do you suggest?" I asked in a quiet voice.

"What do I...*Morgan*." My fake name came out of his mouth as a growl. "You're playing a very dangerous game."

"Is it a game?" I asked. It felt less like a game and more like an inevitable path.

He took my hand in his, lifted it to his mouth. Turning it so my palm faced up, he pressed his mouth against it and inhaled.

A flash of images passed through my mind. Of Adrien's brown eyes, ringed with gold, intent on my mouth as he pulled me close to his chest. In the memory, he was Adrien, not Vosovich. In the memory, he hesitated only a moment before he claimed my lips and stole my breath.

Warmth filled my chest at recovering the lost memory.

"You kissed me," I said.

"Just your hand."

"No. *Before.*"

Darkness filled his eyes. Then he dropped my hand and stepped away so fast I hadn't seen him move. I felt his absence like a chilly breeze, all heat gone.

In a voice just as cool as his absence, he said, "You'll have self-defense tutoring with me on Tuesday at four, and every Tuesday and Thursday after. You'll join my class with the second years in the courtyard."

"I have a meeting with the chancellor then," I said. It was a boring paperwork meeting, just to go over my old transcripts, and I could probably change it, but I felt contrary and wanted to annoy him.

He gave me a false smile. "Then meet me right after. It'll put you here halfway through *mine*."

The way he emphasized the word *mine* made chills march up and down my back. It didn't sound like he was talking about his class.

It sounded like he was making a mating claim.

CHAPTER 7

When I entered Theories of Prophecy on Monday morning, I slid into my seat next to Devon. I waited for him to say something nasty to me, but he didn't tell me it was my fault that he'd gotten in trouble. In fact, he didn't even look at me.

Maybe I wasn't giving him enough credit. It was possible the guy had a little self-control and sense of remorse. If he was happy to leave it alone, so was I.

Professor Thornton floated across the floor in her flowing robes. She'd really nailed the mysterious fortune teller vibe. "As you should already know, prophetic talents are extremely rare, even in the magic community."

I didn't know much about the magic community, but it was a rare manifestation in my family. Generations had passed since the last witch had been born with the ability to see the future. Then Sparrow and I happened. I wasn't entirely convinced it was a gift, like my mother always said. It felt more like a curse.

"My great-grandmother's sister was the last in my family to have the gift," Professor Thornton said. "And I've only run across two oracles in my life. There's something special about their auras."

Her gaze flicked to me, and my cheeks burned. *Please don't call me out. Please don't say my name.*

"But anyone can learn to attune their senses and learn to read auras, just like anyone can read omens in tea leaves. It's a window into a much greater power, a fraction of what some can do, but it's an advantage as much as anything you'll learn in second year Magical Self Defense."

Magical Self Defense, with Professor Adrien Vosovich. I was supposed to join his class tomorrow. He'd insisted on it. I wasn't sure how I felt about that. The flutter in my stomach was half nerves and half excitement. Being close to him lit something inside of me, the same spark I felt with Jace, and with Maxwell. I'd say it was mating instinct if it was just one guy. But three?

"Much like conjuring, to see auras, we must first recognize the energy around us. Close your eyes."

The girl to my left grumbled. I did as I was told and closed my eyes.

"Everyone relax. Listen to the sounds around you, to my voice, to the heart beats of your neighbors, to their slow and easy breathing. In turn, slow your breaths. First inhale until your lungs are full and cold. Exhale until every bit of air has left your lungs. Feel the life around the room, the light that forms a circle. We are all one."

I breathed slowly, unsure how breathing was supposed to make me see auras, but it wasn't the craziest thing that had happened so far. This was Spellbound Academy. Anything was possible.

"In your mind's eye, reach out across the room. Search for a shifter. With your physical eyes closed and your body still, tell me what you see."

"Green." Devon's voice surprised me. I didn't expect someone to answer so quickly, or at all. I only saw black.

"Very good, Mr. Browning," Thornton said. "Those of you who do not see the glow, no need to fret. Keep your eyes closed and try focusing on Poppy. If you are not aware, Ms. Smith is a wolf shifter. Reach across the room and find her, or for another green aura in the room."

It would have helped if I knew who Poppy was. I felt like I was wandering in darkness, while also a bit foolish, since I was just sitting here in my seat.

"I see it," said a voice across the room.

"Me, too," said another.

For me, there was still nothing but black. My nerves fluttered. Only half of us would move on to the second year. I was determined to be one of them. What if I couldn't see auras, something everyone was supposed to be able to do?

Focus. The best thing I could do was focus on my task.

I looked for green in the darkness before realizing I shouldn't be looking for someone else. I should be looking at me. I raised my hands in front of my face and looked with my mind's eye where I knew they should be.

"Others in this room, with talents in different fields of magic should appear—"

"Blue." Devon cut off the professor.

"Very good. Most of us will appear a shade of blue, with our greatest strengths based in common areas of magic."

I was listening, but focused on my hands in front of me. I was a shifter, so there had to be some green light in there somewhere.

"What the hell is that?" Devon's voice tapered off at the end.

I opened my eyes and looked around the room. Everyone was staring at me.

I'd missed something, done something.

Devon leaned closer and squinted at me. "What *are* you?"

"Red." The Professor stared at me, too, unblinking, a wry grin playing on her lips. "Red means Ms. Rose isn't just with us to learn prophecy in theory. She lives it."

There were whispers around the room. All I wanted to do was close my eyes again, hide in the darkness where I couldn't see them all staring. As soon as I did, a vision struck.

A wave of darkness descended over the school and a buzzing sound filled my ears. Everything was obscured in shadow. What did the buzzing mean? I squinted, trying to see through the gloom, and that's when I saw it. The darkness wasn't wispy vapors of shadow—it was formed of millions of bees.

I opened my eyes, completely disoriented.

My head was on a pillow, and I was lying in the middle of the classroom, staring up at the ceiling. Everything was too bright.

I blinked hard.

Fingers tightened around my palm. I looked up and found Jace beside me, holding my hand. "Are you okay?"

"Yeah." I sat up slowly and looked around the room. Everyone was gone except for Professor Thornton, whose stare pinged me in the side of the head like it she was poking a long stick across the room.

"What are you doing here?" I asked Jace.

"I was walking by and heard people leaving the classroom. They said you collapsed."

I squeezed his hand in gratitude.

"This isn't a new power for you," Professor Thornton said. She strolled closer, and I realized I really wanted to be on my feet for this. I felt enough at a disadvantage.

I stood up, and Jace did, too.

"No," I said.

"But you're afraid."

It wasn't a question, so I didn't answer. She could probably read it in my aura or see it in the giant too-open balls that were my eyes.

"I'll help you back to your room." Jace offered me a kind smile, one laced with concern.

"I'm fine, really."

"Whatever happened to you," the professor said, "use it."

"What does that…" What did she mean, use it? She didn't say get over it, or confront it. She said to use it. How was I supposed to *use* my damage?

Jace gently led me to the door and out into the hall. "I bet after some rest you'll feel better."

"No." I stopped walking.

He looked at me, clearly confused.

"I can't miss classes. Besides, I'm fine. Visions just...they happen sometimes. No big deal. I need to go to Conjuring."

"Yeah, okay." He agreed, but I could tell by his tone that he didn't believe me.

* * *

For the first half of Conjuring and Calling, Jace kept looking at me. I appreciated that he cared, but the attention made me uncomfortable. I didn't want him to see me as some kind of fragile flower.

It wasn't until the actual calling part of class started that I felt better. Distraction for the win.

I did as instructed and imagined one of the fuzzy creatures from the forest was sitting on my desk in front of me. So much of my experience with magic in Spellbound was centered around manifestation. Make it happen with force of will. If only that worked on visions, like it used to.

Lapinfées popped up all around the room, fluffy little

balls of fur with fairy-like wings and rabbit ears. But mine refused to come. I needed to concentrate. Breathe, focus.

I closed my eyes and inhaled slowly, imagining lush, airy blue fur. Imagining little beady eyes darting to and fro, and long ears twitching to the sides at every noise.

With an exhale, I told myself I was holding one in my palms.

And I believed.

I could feel her rapid heartbeat, smell her floral scent.

I opened my eyes. The lapinfée fluttered up out of my palm and up into the air with the others before landing on my shoulder. She had a white spot between her eyes and a torn ear. This was the same lapinfée I'd seen at the bonfire. I did it!

"Good job, Morgan." Jace touched my other shoulder, and I turned.

There was a lapinfée on his head, and two more on top of that. I laughed. "So I guess you called one, too. Or three."

He shrugged. "Seems like I did."

I SNATCHED a seat in the back of the room in Philosophy of Magic and managed to stay out of the debate during class. I took a ton of notes on the pros and cons of setting aside the ancient "harm none" precept if harming some would be for the good of all.

But the whole time, I could feel Maxwell's strong gaze set on me. It seared, and I couldn't wait to escape.

As soon as class was over, I made a break for the stairs, but a firm hand grabbed my wrist. I didn't have to turn to know who it belonged to. The heat that spread from his touch was enough.

Everyone else escaped, leaving me alone in the classroom with Maxwell Phillips.

I didn't know what he wanted. He probably blamed me for the kissing game, and for getting attacked by the Guardian. We hadn't spoken about either, or about how we knew each other, or about anything really. I liked it like that. I wanted to leave it like that.

"Tell me why you're here," he said.

I spun on my heel and held my head high. "Because you're grabbing my arm."

He looked down, furrowed his brows, and let go.

I rubbed my hand over the place where I could still feel him on my skin. I could taste cinnamon on my tongue, even though we were two feet apart and the last thing I wanted to do was kiss this man who hated me.

"Why are you at Spellbound Academy, Wren? Why are you lying about your name?"

I frowned and met his gaze. It was cold steel. How could one man be so hot and so cold at the same time?

"I shouldn't—"

"Trust me."

"Yeah, that." I shook my head. "I can't. How could I when you look at me like that?"

"Like what?"

"Like you want to tear my clothes off and shove me away at the same time." I couldn't believe I'd said the words out loud. My cheeks heated.

Maxwell straightened his shoulders and looked at me like he couldn't believe I'd said it either. "I don't…"

His eyes softened, only for a moment, before his lips crushed mine.

He tasted like cinnamon and regret, bruising before he pulled away. I was breathless and confused as ever. He ran his fingers through his dirty-blond hair and paced.

"You're my mate, Wren."

I sighed. Maxwell, Jace, and Adrien. I said nothing.

"I've known since I met you, hell, since I first laid eyes on you. I haven't stopped thinking about our night together since you left. I've never felt this way about anyone, and I can't breathe without you near. I've been fucking dead inside, Wren. You can trust me."

I believed him that I could trust him, and I felt like shit. I wasn't sure what to say in return—that I was sorry? I was, even though I shouldn't have been. It was him who'd pushed me away, him who wouldn't let me kiss him that night under the stars in Emerald Pines.

"You say that we're mates," I said, "that you've always known. But what you did…"

"I couldn't. I wanted to. I wanted you, more than anything. But you weren't healed. Not after what Curtis had done. It hurt like hell pushing you away. I was trying to protect you, waiting until you were well enough to make that decision."

He'd been right to do that. Thinking back, I could remember what a wreck I'd been. In some ways, I was still broken. But as far as my mind, and healing from the trauma, I was well. At least, well enough to choose a mate.

Or three.

But I had no words. I had to leave. However, the least I could do was give him the answer that he asked for. He'd asked me why I was lying about my name. That was an answer I could give him. "I had a vision."

He stopped pacing and looked at me.

"They're always about other people," I said, "but this time it was different. Something dark is coming...for me."

"I'll protect you."

"I'm not looking for a bodyguard. I want to learn to grow stronger. I'm tired of being hounded and followed. I want anyone who comes for me to know that I won't be taken again. I *will* defend myself."

Reaching out, he cupped my chin in his hand. "You're one of the strongest people I know."

I gripped his wrist, hard, tempted to push him away from me like he'd done to me that night. But the adoring look in his eyes prevented it. I wanted nothing more than to kiss him, but I'd been shot down once. I didn't want to risk that again.

"I'm never going to reject you again," he said in a low voice, then dipped his head to mine.

The kiss was full of a languid, lava-like passion. Slowly flowing yet burning everything in its wake.

Before I could think about what I was doing, I moved my hands along the front of his shirt, undoing button after button. He pressed into me so I could feel his hardness against my lower belly. I wanted it lower, wanted to feel him everywhere.

Just as I placed my hands against the bare skin of his chest, I remembered where we were.

We could *not* get naked in the Philosophy of Magic classroom.

I pulled away.

Maxwell smirked.

"Why didn't you stop me?" I asked.

He shrugged. "I told you I wouldn't reject you ever again."

I snorted. "Yeah, that would be really helpful if I were to get expelled for...for indecency."

"Aw, people have been caught doing worse, I'm sure."

I watched as Maxwell buttoned his shirt, appreciating his flex of muscles as much as how he hadn't wanted to go back on his word about not rejecting me. I wanted to tell him more about my feelings, but I wasn't sure how to word them. I could screw things up, just by admitting how I felt.

But secrets were a terrible way to start a relationship.

"I have to tell you something," I said.

He stopped buttoning his shirt and looked straight at me.

"I feel the same as you," I said. "I think you're it. But I'm not sure what it means, when I have similar feelings...for someone else."

"Ah."

It was an infuriatingly simple sound. It meant nothing. I waited, hoping he'd elaborate, but he just watched me.

A loud popping sound broke the silence between us, and a lapinfée appeared from nowhere. With a damaged ear and a white spot between her eyes, I recognized the lapinfée as the one I had conjured in class, the one from the forest. She landed on Maxwell's shoulder and chomped down on his collar.

"Get off." He batted a hand at her.

The lapinfée flew up and missed his swipe.

I laughed.

"You're going to laugh instead of help me?" Maxwell frowned.

"Help you? She's a sweet little ball of fuzz."

He looked down at his shoulder and pulled on his collar. His frown deepened. "She destroyed my shirt."

"Destroyed? No way." I took a step closer and inspected the damage. And okay, maybe she tore it a little.

"Why is it here?" he asked.

"I think she likes me."

"That's ridiculous."

"I called her in Conjuring class."

His blue eyes weighed my expression and he took a step closer to me. A set of long blue ears rose over Maxwell's shoulder.

He turned and the lapinfée swung with him, attached to his collar by her teeth.

"Tell it to *go*," he said.

I shrugged. "I don't know how."

He shook his head. "It might like you, but it doesn't like me."

"I don't know," I said. "Maybe that's just how she shows affection."

He snorted. "Little terror."

"I think I'm going to call her Nibbles." Nibbles flew over and landed on my shoulder. She snuggled her soft bunny face into the crook of my neck. It tickled and I smiled.

Maxwell glared at her then met my gaze once again and took my hand. "Call it what you want. But Wren, I want you to remember I'm here for you. No matter what happens, or what's coming, I'll be here."

"Thank you." I planted a quick peck on his cheek before turning for the door. It felt like too little after what we'd just shared, but with that kiss, I'd shown him how I felt even if I hadn't told him. If we were really supposed to be mates, we had our entire lives for me to figure it out.

Lost in thought, I meandered back toward my room, with Nibbles still on my shoulder making the occasional clicking sound.

When I reached the library, my stomach started to churn and sweat formed on my palms. My heart beat faster, blood pulsing in my ears, and a sense of dread overwhelmed everything else.

Cora was nearby. I reached for her, but she wasn't close enough, and besides, she was talking to someone—a woman in a business suit with blond hair and her back turned to me. Cora's happiness was at odds with the feeling of despair filling my gut.

I backed up, my shoulders slamming into the wall, and I looked around, expecting a nasty vision to overtake me. I folded over, trying to figure out what was wrong with me.

Looking for Cora again, I saw tendrils of darkness coiled up her legs. Fear pulsed through my veins. I wanted to call out to Cora, but she was still talking to the woman.

It was a vision, but not. Cora was clearly there, and the woman with her. But I was seeing more than what was present in the hallway.

I tried to focus, to see what this vision was telling me.

The shadowy spirals were coming from the woman in the suit.

There wasn't anything wrong with me. It was *her*. There was something wrong with the woman talking to Cora.

CHAPTER 8

It had taken me over an hour to settle down after the weird vision in the hallway. I figured the best thing would be to study until Cora returned. Nibbles distracted me with her clicking sounds as I pored through my books, until she finally got bored and fluttered off.

After a few more minutes of me staring blankly at a book, the door to my dorm room banged open, and Cora said, "Now that is the sexiest thing I've ever seen."

I looked up from the books spread out on my desk. "What is?"

"Books. Studying. So. Hot."

I laughed, grabbed a throw pillow from my bed, and tossed it at her. She caught it easily and tossed it back on the bed.

"Hey, I wanted to talk to you," I said, feeling suddenly nervous. She'd looked so happy when talking to that woman, I didn't want to ruin whatever feelings she had about it.

"I wanted to talk to you, too," she said. "You would not believe who spoke to me today."

Crap.

"Well," I said slowly, "I saw you talking to that blond woman in the hall outside of the library."

"Yes!" Cora clapped her hands and dropped her bulging messenger bag on her desk, where several other books slid to the floor, displaced.

I'd never seen her treat a book with anything other than reverence, so this spoke to her distraction.

"That woman is the rockstar of the shifter world," Cora said. "She is the richest and runs the lead business in...well, everything. And she talked to *me*. Me!"

"That's great," I said, forcing the words out in a rush, "but I should tell you about this thing—"

"She said she's very interested in seeing my end-of-term presentation, and she's looking to bring another lion shifter into her family. That's what she calls her company, Morgan. Her *family*. It's not just a business to her, it's a passion project. And belonging with them, well, it's pretty much the opportunity everyone dreams of."

Her slate-green eyes were glazed with excitement, her cheeks flushed. I'd never seen Cora so jubilant. I remembered what Jace had told me about the corporations and Cora's dream to be the first in her family to be chosen to join one.

"I can't study tonight," she said. "I need to go tell Blake and Thomas."

She grabbed her tube of purple lipstick from the edge of her desk and walked to the mirror on the door.

"Wait, Cora, just a second," I said.

She looked at me through the mirror, her eyebrows raised, the purple lippy nearly touching her mouth. "What is it?"

"I, well, I hate to say any of this, but I have a really bad feeling about that woman."

"Charlize?" Her hand fell away from her mouth, lipstick forgotten.

"Yeah," I said.

Cora came over and perched on the edge of my desk, looking down at me. Her gaze was trusting, but surprised. "What do you mean?"

I took a deep breath. "You don't know this about me, but I have visions. And this thing happened, right before I came to Spellbound. The vision was awful, left me feeling sick and weak. And I had one again when I saw you talking to that woman in the hall today."

"Okay," Cora said. "What else?"

"That's...it," I said slowly. "That's all. Just the vision, the bad feeling in my gut."

It paled in comparison to her glee at having talked to Charlize. I could see Cora's thoughts flit over her face. A little bit of reservation, quickly overcome by how starstruck she'd been.

"It doesn't seem like much," I said. "But the feeling is real. My visions used to be very dependable."

Well, that had been the wrong thing to say. *Used to be very dependable*. I sounded like a total flake.

Cora nodded. "Okay. Thanks for telling me."

I touched her wrist. "Will you think about it, at least? Even though I know you don't believe me?"

"We don't need to talk about it anymore," she said. "I still want to go spend some time with Blake and Thomas."

"Right, okay," I said.

She set the tube of lipstick down on her desk and left.

* * *

THE NEXT DAY WAS TUESDAY—MY first lesson with Adrien. I knew I'd be late because of going through some paperwork with the chancellor. I wished Adrien had told me I could skip this week and come the following, but it wasn't a surprise he hadn't given me the out.

The sounds of people sparring reached my ears before I'd even set foot in the courtyard. Adrien's special second-year class was, as expected, already in progress. I stood off to the side, close to the corner of his office, trying to stay out of sight while I took in the scene before me.

While some of the fighting was magical, most of it was physical. I shouldn't have expected less from another wolf shifter. Our bodies were our best weapons.

Cora and a red-haired guy conjured balls of light and hurled them at each other. Every time they missed, the ball would sail into one of the walls and make a little puff of smoke. Every time they landed on their target, a glowing green spatter would appear on their clothes.

"Good thing we're filling these with aura boogers instead of a sleeping spell," Cora said as her last ball made contact.

Adrien worked with two guys, correcting their stances and showing them, in slow motion, how to throw punches that came from the hips and abdomen, not the arms. My dad had taught me a lot of that stuff already.

I missed my dad. Mom, too. I'd have to call them as soon as I was able. Maybe I could call over Thanksgiving break.

"Ms. Rose." Adrien's deep voice seemed to cut right through to my heart. "Thank you for joining us."

"Thanks for having me," I said.

"So polite," Cora muttered.

I shot her a look, and she grinned.

"Where are your leggings?" Adrien asked.

I looked more closely at everyone and noticed all the women had leggings on underneath their uniform skirts.

"There's an extra pair in my bag over there," Cora said,

nodding to a row of backpacks and bags lined up next to Adrien's office.

"Thanks," I told her, and went to her messenger bag.

Inside, I found the leggings. When I pulled them out, an envelope came with them with Cora's name in an elegant script. When my hands made contact with the paper, a strong sense of dread came over me.

Not another vision. Not here.

I bit my lip hard enough to taste blood, then dropped the envelope back into Cora's bag and went into Adrien's office to pull on the leggings so I didn't flash the entire class.

Before stepping out of the office, I took another moment to watch the students sparring. Three giant guys were taking turns going into pairs. Was Adrien going to make me spar with one of them? They'd kick my ass so fast.

"Are you going to join us, Ms. Rose?" Adrien called.

He was looking right at me, where I was staring through the glass window of his office door like a peeping Tom.

Face burning, I stepped back into the courtyard, smoothing my skirt and making sure it wasn't tucked into the leggings, because that was the last thing I needed.

"Ms. Rose," Adrien said, pointing between me and Cora, "you can spar with Ms. Gladstone. Ms. Gladstone, please show her how to form the energy missiles."

The idea of energy missiles would have freaked me the hell out if I hadn't seen that they just looked like balls of light, like the one we'd thrown around in the woods.

I walked over to my roommate, relieved. Cora's eyes twinkled as she conjured a ball of green light in her palm.

"So," she said, "the thing is, you can't just toss the energy like you're playing a kissing game in the woods."

I made a face at her. "Great...but what *is* the energy?"

"Oh, it's a part of your aura."

Excitement bubbled in my stomach. "Ooh, I can see it! This is great."

"Actually...I think everyone can see it when it's been pulled from an aura. It doesn't have the same protection as it does when it's attached to your spirit. Or some metaphysical mumbo-jumbo like that." She grinned.

Disappointed, I nodded. "It explains why some people are throwing green balls, and others are throwing blue balls."

She snickered, and I fought back a giggle because I could feel Adrien's gaze on us, even though I couldn't see where he was looking.

"Once you pull the piece of your aura off of you, you put it in a conjured ball of light. It sounds like a lot of steps, but it can happen immediately. Go ahead, give it a try."

I couldn't see my aura...did that mean I wouldn't be able to grab a part of it? Heart thumping because of the people around us—people I definitely didn't want to fail in front of —I felt for the protective aura around my body. It was there. I couldn't see it, but I could feel it. I imagined pulling a piece of it away. It didn't hurt—I didn't even notice its loss. It was as if my aura regenerated the missing part immediately.

"I got it," I said.

"Good," she said. "Now put it in a ball."

I did as she asked, conjuring a ball and feeling the intensity of my willpower shoving the piece of my aura inside. Next thing I knew, I held a red ball of glowing light in my palm.

"Great job," Cora said.

I smiled, pleased with myself.

"There's more to it than aim," she continued with her satisfied little grin. "There's intent, and there's speed. So what you've done is conjure some aural energy, not from the world, but from yourself—just harmless stuff—and you're going to try to hit me with it."

I tossed the ball in my hand, liking how the reddish light flickered and moved within it.

"Now," she said, "I want you to thrust it forward not as a throw, but a push. And your intent is to hit me with it."

I tried it out, and missed, but she clapped anyway. I was grateful everyone else seemed absorbed in their own exercises. Adrien stood at the other end of the courtyard, arms crossed, his eyes hidden behind sunglasses. I couldn't tell if he was watching me or not, which was for the best. I needed to focus. Cora encouraged me, and I tried a few more times before everything clicked and I actually hit her.

After a while, Adrien had Cora switch places with another girl, Juliana. She didn't go nearly as easy on me and I got hit a few times with her magic, which splattered me with green goo.

I practiced with her until Adrien said, "That's it, everyone. Class is dismissed."

I hurried over to the line of backpacks along the courtyard wall, but Adrien said, "Ms. Morgan, you will remain here."

I stopped in my tracks and turned to face him. "Why?"

It was impossible to see his eyes behind those damn sunglasses. "You were half an hour late," he said, "so you owe me half an hour."

A half hour with Adrien Vosovich? I was so ready for that.

Cora was the last of everyone else to leave, and she gave me a wave and mouthed, *Don't be polite.*

I laughed and waved back.

And then it was just me and Adrien. I looked down at myself, feeling disgusted—I was covered in magical boogers.

"Show me what you learned here today," he said.

No preamble, no asking how it went. All business. Fine, I could do that. Conjuring up a ball of energy, I pushed it outward to one of the gargoyles lining the courtyard walls.

The ball of light exploded harmlessly over stone. Nodding in satisfaction, I turned back to see that Adrien had a ball of his own light, ready and waiting in his hand.

"Good, you can direct the magic outward," he said. "But can you evade an attack?"

"No," I said. "That's one of the things I want to learn." If I'd known it, maybe Curtis wouldn't have been able to kidnap me so easily. Why hadn't Mom and Dad sent me here before? Did they think I wasn't strong enough to handle it? Probably. They'd always coddled me, they'd always thought me sweet and impressionable.

No more.

"You can deflect magic with magic," Adrien said, "but that isn't my area of expertise. I can barely conjure this ball of light because the witch power in me is so diluted. But you can also evade it physically. Like me, you have an advantage with physical evasion because you're also a shifter. So that's what we're going to work on now."

I nodded, eyeing the ball of light he held with some trepidation. It was green, like I imagined his wolf shifter aura would be.

"If you hit me with that, what's it going to do?" I asked.

"No idea. Try not to get hit so you don't find out the hard way." He grinned and I nearly fell over with shock. Had I ever seen Adrien smile?

Without warning, he hurled the ball in my direction. I leapt to the side, felt the energy of it whoosh past my elbow. Close call.

"You have to do more than dodge," Adrien said. "You have to anticipate."

Already he held a new ball of light, and he tossed it up in the air. Quicker than I could see, he threw it at me. I spun and crouched, avoiding it once more, then was up and facing him. He threw another ball, which I also dodged, but another was sailing at me before I could recover. I ducked and rolled to the side before jumping to my feet again.

"That wasn't fair," I said. "You didn't give me time to—"

Another ball was coming for me, and a second after that. I didn't have time to evade both of them. The second light hit me square in the chest and I felt my eyes fly wide open in surprise. At the same time, a liquid heat filled my body. I rubbed my thighs together.

Want. Desire.

Adrien was right there, looking tall and strong and capable. We were alone in the courtyard. What was to stop us from acting on this overpowering feeling of need?

He held another ball of light, ready to throw, but he froze at the sight of me. "Ms. Rose?"

I walked toward him, my steps sultry, and I played with the top button on my shirt.

The ball of light in his hand winked out and disappeared.

"Fuck," he said. "Morgan, what you're feeling right now, that isn't you."

"Don't care," I said, only stopping my advance when we were face to face. "I want you, Adrien."

He held his arms straight down at his sides, and his hands were curled into fists. "You don't understand. I was scooping energy from my aura, and you got hit with my feelings."

Running my hands over my chest, stomach, and hips, I said, "So this is what you're feeling right now, too? For me?"

He nodded. "I didn't realize it would transfer over. We can get the chancellor or Professor Thornton out here to figure it out right away. I'm so sorry. Only strong emotions get passed on, and I wasn't thinking of one of the strongest ones of all—desire. Worst I thought could happen was you would get some of my fatigue from not sleeping last night..."

I only picked up one important piece of information—he felt this way about me, too. That was all it took, right? Two people wanting each other. I wrapped my arms around his neck and twined one of my legs around his, plastering myself to the front of his body.

"Adrien," I whispered, "I feel this way, too."

He slowly reached up, grabbed my wrists, and pulled my arms from around his neck. "No, you don't," he said, "or we would've been doing more of this from the beginning."

"I do," I insisted. Was he rejecting me, like Maxwell had done? Except he said I was feeling what he felt. So this wasn't rejection...it was something else. I didn't want to think about it too hard. "And I don't want to fight it anymore."

He looked around. "It'll fade in a few minutes. Take some deep breaths, okay? Let's go inside."

Did he want me inside, where I couldn't make a fool of myself in the full light of day? Hell, I wasn't ashamed of my feelings for Adrien. Let everyone see. Let the chancellor see.

But the office would be more private, and maybe I could convince him to take the next, natural step with me. I went limp, hoping to lull him into a false sense of security. Somehow, I had to convince him that this was the right thing to do. We both wanted it—what were we waiting for?

"Good," he said, "it's already wearing off." It sounded almost like a lie, but not quite. If I wasn't preoccupied by the consuming feeling of need spiraling in my lower abdomen, I might have tried to puzzle it out.

He led me to the office and had me sit in the chair in front of his desk. I noticed he'd left the door open, but that was fine. It was Tuesday evening, classes were over, and nobody would be coming around.

He stood in front of me, leaning back against his desk. His eyes were still hidden behind those sunglasses, but his mouth was twisted in disappointment.

I didn't want him to be sad or disappointed. I wanted him

to be happy. I wanted him to shout in ecstasy while he came in tandem with me. So I tackled him.

He gave an *oof* of surprise and his arms came around me automatically. He cupped my ass and I felt his hardness, rigid between my legs. I pressed my lips to his and this time, he kissed me back for a blissful moment of tongues, lips, and teeth before pulling away, gasping.

"Wren," he said. "We can't."

He pried me off of him and set me in the chair again. I pouted up at him, loving the way he groaned in response.

"You're killing me," he said. "Don't make me tie you to that chair."

That was a good idea. I nodded eagerly.

Shaking his head, he stepped back. "The effects of my aura should wear off you at any moment, and then we're going to talk."

Slowly, the all-encompassing need I'd felt moments ago was draining away. I chased its loss, saddened not because it was gone, but because the intensity was fading. Yet my own feelings—what I felt for Adrien all the time—they were still right where I'd left them, slowly burning.

I stared up at him. "Take off your sunglasses."

He tilted his head slightly, considering, then removed the blasted things from his face.

Now, now I could see the fiery gold of his gaze, the turmoil and restraint battling within.

"So," he said. "Now you see it, don't you? You just got a dose of my aura. What do you think?"

I struggled to remember some of what he'd said moments ago in the courtyard and pieced it together with this. "You mean—I got hit with the strength of your feelings? That's how you feel *all the time*?"

"For you, yes," he said.

I wanted him just as badly. Supposedly the effects were

wearing off, but I still wanted him. I was in control, though, not attacking him like the shameless hussy of a wolf who lived inside me wanted to do. How did he control himself? No wonder he was such a grump.

"You know some friends of mine," he said.

"Isn't that a little off topic?" I asked.

He grinned again. I really liked his grin. It was self-deprecating and sexy at the same time. "Not really. Hear me out."

"Okay. Who are these friends?"

"Slade Rouland is one of them. He and I go way back, to the war in Badinor."

I remembered Slade—too well. He was one of the dragon shifters who'd rescued me from Curtis's tower. I'd been filthy, reeking of my own despair. The world around me had darkened, my visions overtaking me because I refused to prophesy anything for Curtis.

"They were worried when you disappeared on them," Adrien said.

"I felt bad about that," I said. But I'd needed to run. Curtis might've been gone, but I didn't need to be an oracle to follow my gut and know that I was still in danger. And when Sparrow had gotten in touch...I knew I had to leave.

"I'll get in touch with them over Thanksgiving," Adrien said, "and without giving them any details, I'll let them know you're okay."

"Thanks," I said.

"Also," he said, "I met your sister. She's the reason I'm here at Spellbound. She told me that when I came here, I'd find my mate."

"And...that's me?" I asked.

"It's the only thing that can explain why I'm so drawn to you, Wren. The only explanation for the way my chest tightens whenever you're around, like some kind of rope is dragging me to you and I can't resist."

I felt it, too. I felt it now. But there was something he needed to know.

"You're not the only one," I blurted.

He blinked, slowly, shuttering those gorgeous brown eyes before opening them again. "I gathered that. The friendly kitten, right?"

It took me a second to realize who he meant.

"Jace," I said. "He's a mountain lion shifter. Don't be petty."

There was that grin again.

I continued, "And it's Maxwell, too. Maybe. I don't know, I don't understand any of this."

"I don't mind sharing if they don't...as long as I get some time with you. Either alone, or," he paused, his eyes flashing with desire, "all together. That is something I'd very much like to see."

CHAPTER 9

Weeks and months passed without my getting attacked by Guardians, or without any incidents at all. I studied, flirted with Jace, Maxwell, and Adrien in turn, and fell into an exhausted sleep every night. Thanksgiving happened, and Christmas. At each one, I was allowed to call my parents. I didn't leave the grounds though, so I couldn't even attempt to reach Sparrow through a vision. If I'd had a phone number for her, I'd have called her, too. But our parents didn't even know how to get in touch with her, so it was looking like I'd have to wait until summer.

I didn't have any visions over those months. No darkness, no bees. Even if I didn't need the defense classes for safety, I was really enjoying the time with Adrien. Since our *talk*, Maxwell didn't look at me the same way. His gaze was still heated, but never with hatred. And Jace offered to tutor me in the areas I just couldn't seem to figure out, like reading auras. Fridays were group bonfires, and on Saturdays, I belonged to Jace.

"Close your eyes."

My eyes fluttered shut, quick to obey. I could still feel him in front of me, his legs crossed only a few inches from mine on the hard dorm room floor. Without sight, my attention switched to my other senses, just as it did every time we tried this.

His dusty, feline scent filled my lungs. I listened to his slow, steady heartbeat, each inhale and exhale. From sound and scent alone I could envision him sitting there watching me, with a playful sparkle in his eyes even while we weren't playing at all. It was just the way he looked at me, and I loved that.

But, I wasn't supposed to be thinking about boyish grins, or how fantastic Jace looked without his shirt. I was supposed to be looking for color. One color in particular—green. As a shifter, Jace's aura was green. Or at least that's what everyone else told me. All I ever saw was black.

"I'm starting to think I'm psychically colorblind." I squinted to watch his reaction.

Jace put his hand on my thigh and squeezed. "No peeking."

Warmth spread from the contact, and I found myself wanting more. Not more practice, more of Jace. I closed my eyes like he told me to.

"It can't be a part of the finals, can it?" I asked. "A bunch of people line up and I have to tell them what color they are?"

"It's impossible to know what they'll ask of you. It's different every year."

"Too bad it's not just a written test." I leaned back on my palms and opened my eyes. "I would nail it."

"Magical theory only goes so far," Jace said. "You have to be able to put what you're taught into practice, or what's the point? And you'll master reading auras, just like you master everything else. You make conjuring look easy, something the rest of us have been practicing for years."

"Nothing feels easy."

"Would it be worth it if it did, Morgan?"

I looked over his kind face and considered his question. Would I still be here if learning magic was easy? Yes, probably. But it wouldn't mean as much. And the same went for figuring out my feelings. It wasn't easy to navigate the minefield of having three mates, but giving up wasn't an option. Deep down I knew Maxwell, Adrien, and Jace were all meant to be with me. And figuring out what happened next was as exciting as it was intimidating.

I shrugged and offered a non-committal maybe.

One thing had been bothering me, though—Jace still thought I was Morgan Rose, not Wren Solaris. It didn't feel right, hearing my fake name coming from his lips. And it wasn't that I didn't trust him, because I trusted him with my life. It was that I didn't know how to break the news that I wasn't who he'd thought I was.

I also wanted to come clean to Cora, but first, I had to start with her brother.

"Hey, there's something I want to tell you," I said.

"Sure, go for it." Jace leaned back into the bedframe. As he did, the bed jarred, and a piece of paper fell to the floor.

"What's this?" He picked it up.

The envelope had a waxed seal on the back. With the flap closed, the seal was plainly visible—a bee.

"Don't." I knew exactly what it was. I could feel it. It was the envelope from Cora's bag, the one that made my stomach sink. And that bee linked this feeling to my vision. If only I knew exactly what the danger was.

"Don't what?" Jace turned it over in his hands, then pulled out the paper inside.

"There's something wrong with that letter," I said.

"It looks like it's been read about a thousand times. If it was cursed, I'd be dead by now. Or I'd have two heads." He made a move like he was going to open it, but he was watching me instead of looking at the paper.

"It's not mine," I blurted. "It's Cora's."

Jace frowned.

"You know that vision that I had in Prophecy, the first week of school?"

"The one you didn't want to talk about? Where I found you on the floor? How could I forget?"

I nodded. "There's a darkness, and bees. Something bad is coming for me and I have a feeling it's related to a woman I saw in the hall at the beginning of the year, and to this letter."

"What do you mean?"

"I...it's hard to explain, but I just know it's related. And she's interested in hiring Cora."

Jace's frown grew deeper and he opened the letter.

"Wait, don't—"

He read, *"Dear Ms. Gladstone, I wanted to tell you how impressed I was with your first-year exam performance. I am very interested in seeing how you do after your final year at Spellbound Academy."*

I moved in next to him and looked at the paper. *We're always looking to add magically-skilled shifters to our family.*

"What are you doing?" Cora's mouth hung open and she ran over and snatched the letter from Jace.

"We were just…" I trailed off. "It fell down when—"

"I don't know what's gotten into you, Morgan, but this is messed up. Stay out of my business."

"I'm sor—"

"I'm the one who opened it," Jace said. "But that isn't the point. If Morgan says this woman is bad news, then Geard isn't to be trusted."

"Seriously, Jace? You know who Geard is. And you're going to side with...you know what? I'm done." Cora started gathering her books in her arms. "I'm staying with Blake tonight."

I rose to my feet, and reached for her shoulder. "Look, Cora—"

She pulled away. "Don't. Just give me my space. Please."

I wanted to grab her shoulders and tell her to stay away from Charlize Geard, that I cared about her. But I knew that I wasn't being fair to her. So I let her go.

"She never stays mad for long," Jace said. "Don't worry."

I was all kinds of worried. I didn't want her to be angry with me, but I also didn't want her to be in danger.

* * *

I DIDN'T SEE Cora on Sunday. I decided it was best to give her space like she wanted while I figured out the best way to articulate my concern. I didn't want to push her away further, but I couldn't just let it go.

Classes went by in a blur, and it wasn't until Defense class that I saw Cora again.

Adrien assigned me as her partner, and when I stood across from her and looked into her eyes, I found her uncharacteristically cold, colder than the icy chill in the air. How pissed was she at me?

Jace had said she never stays mad for long, but maybe it hadn't been long enough.

A high-pitched whistle signaled that we were meant to start.

I glanced at Adrien, whistle in his mouth, eyes on me. As I turned back, I caught a glimpse of bright green just in time to get covered in gooey green mess.

Cora laughed from somewhere beyond the slime.

"Don't be polite, right?" I laughed.

I rubbed away the goo from my face and saw a big ball floating between her swaying hands.

"Exactly." The smile on her face told me she wasn't as angry with me as she'd first seemed. Or maybe covering me in magical boogers was all the reconciliation she needed. Whatever the reason, I was glad things between us seemed to be back to normal.

"Better focus." Cora winked at me and lobbed a giant green ball my way.

My instinct wasn't to create magic of my own, but to dodge. I charged her, ducking under the green ball without stopping. My foot slipped on icy stone, but I didn't falter.

"Nice!" Cora backpedaled, then turned on her heel and wove between two of the guys lined up beside her.

Smart. I couldn't hit her without risking hitting them.

A ball of white light whizzed over my head, and I ducked just in time to dodge one of the balls the guys were throwing at each other. The gate at the edge of the wall was open, and for a moment, I seemed to have lost her. But I listened to the courtyard. Frost filled my lungs as I breathed in, searching for the dusty scent of lion. She hadn't left the area. She was still here.

This time, when Cora threw a ball, I was ready.

The green glob barreled right at my back, but I spun around and I wasn't sure how I knew, but I did. I imagined a mirror, a reflective shield of light stolen from the energy of the magic all around the room.

And the ball bounced back, splattering Cora.

I looked around the courtyard, and it wasn't just the one she'd thrown that had rebounded, but all the magic that had been thrown splattered back against those who had cast it.

"How did you do that?" Cora ran over to me, looking like she'd climbed through a mountain of green gelatin.

"I'm not sure."

"Well, figure it out," she said, "because you have to show me."

I laughed. "Yeah, I'll try."

Adrien was standing there, his eyes covered in those sunglasses, his arms crossed highlighting the strength and size of his muscles. "Good work, Ms. Rose."

"Thanks," I said.

"Back to it." He waved a hand at the class, and everyone stopped staring and returned to their exercises.

"Can we talk a minute?" Cora touched my elbow.

I nodded and followed her to the side of the courtyard.

Her greenish-gray eyes were serious. "I miss you."

"I miss you, too," I said.

"Let's put this whole thing behind us."

"I'd like that."

"Can we just promise not to talk about Charlize?"

I bit my lip, holding back all the warnings I wanted to give her. I wouldn't give up on trying to protect her, but I needed my best friend. Maybe it was selfish of me, but I didn't want to deny her and lose her friendship. "Yes. I can do that."

"Thanks, Morgan." She threw her arms around me.

Wren. I wanted to tell her my name was Wren. The longer I went without telling her and Jace the truth, the worse I felt. But we'd just made up over the Charlize issue. I wanted to feel normal for a little while at least, for as long as I could.

AFTER CLASS, I waited to see if I could talk to Adrien. Most of the second-years headed out of the courtyard, chattering as they went. They seemed to have mastered a spell for making the magical aura boogers disappear. I'd have to ask Cora about it later.

Unfortunately, two of the guys were intent on talking to Adrien about something, so I gave him a little wave, gathered my things, and returned to the building.

I felt relieved about making up with Cora, but also gross. Being covered in magical aura boogers could do that to a person. As soon as I reached the dorms, I grabbed a change of clothes and my toiletries and headed into the girls' showers.

One step inside, and I started to gag. The air was filled with some kind of noxious blue gas. A girl with black hair ran out shielding her nose and mouth in the crook of her elbow. She keeled over and coughed.

"You okay?" I asked.

When she looked up at me, I got a good look at her face. Margaret Rodriguez. I barely recognized her with her eyes nearly swollen shut. Her room was across the hall from mine, and she was in my Conjuring and Calling class.

"Yep. Great. But, uh, don't go in there."

"What happened?"

"Spell gone wrong. It'll clear out...in a day or two. I'd use the guys' bathroom. If you don't want to end up with this." She lifted her sleeve, revealing giant welts.

"Let's get you to the nurse's off—"

"Nope. I'm totally fine, really. Just pretend you didn't see me here. That's all the help I need."

"Uh, sure. Okay. If you promise to leave up a sign so no one else goes in by accident."

"Deal."

Margaret ran off before returning with a piece of paper and pen for a sign, and I crossed the hall to the men's room. I knocked on the wall outside, called in a warning that a chick was coming, and waited for a response before stepping in.

Lucky for me, it was completely empty. I'd hoped for as much in the early evening.

I took the last shower area at the end, pulled the flimsy curtain closed, and turned on the water. Here I'd have at least a little privacy if someone came in.

My uniform was plastered to my skin, so peeling it off was a job and a half. But as the warm water washed over me, everything else melted away. I closed my eyes and leaned into the water. It streamed down my face and over my body. It smelled like rain, with a kick of dust to it, and I breathed in and out, relishing the scent.

A deep voice pulled me from my thoughts. "Morgan?"

I screamed, tried to cover myself with my hands, and backed toward the corner of the stall, as far from the voice as possible.

But when I blinked away the water, I saw who was there. Jace, standing on the other side of the low curtain.

"Can I come in?" he asked.

I nodded. I should have known sooner. I should have known he was here as soon as I'd noticed his dusty scent.

He stepped into the stall with me, wearing nothing but a towel.

"Hi." My face heated, meaning I was probably as red as my towel that was sitting on the bench. I gave it a glance, debating whether I should make a move for it.

"What are you doing in here?" A smile played on his lips. "Not that I'm complaining."

My first thought was to ask him what *he* was doing here, but this was the men's room. Instead, I answered. "The women's room is out of commission. You don't mind sharing, do you?"

Why did I say it like that? Flashes of being hit with Adrien's feelings passed through my head, the bruising feel of Maxwell's kiss. I wanted them both. And I wanted Jace.

"With you, Morgan?" He took a step closer, and water ran

down his bare, sculpted chest, soaking the towel that clung to his hips. "Never."

I lowered my hands in invitation. He took another step closer, and another, so we were only inches apart. His wild scent surrounded me. His green eyes were fire, and I wanted to touch him, to feel him, to kiss him.

He bent down and claimed my mouth with his, first gentle and slow, then harder and more desperate. The tension I'd been holding onto washed away, not like it had in the water, but more. I was safe with Jace. I didn't need to hide, not from the world, not from him. I wanted him here in the shower. Now.

But his words repeated in my head. He'd called me *Morgan.*

I couldn't do this, not without telling him first.

I pulled back and leaned my head on the tile. I met his gaze, and I didn't know how he would take it, but I had to tell him.

"Wren," I whispered. "My name is Wren."

"Wren," he repeated. It was a song on his tongue.

I expected him to be angry, to walk away, but he didn't.

"I wanted to tell you sooner," I said. "I wanted to tell you when—"

He stole my words and my breath with his kiss. I belonged to him, and he belonged to me. We were mates, even if what he knew about me was built on lies. He wanted me anyway.

I ran my fingers over him, learning the muscles of his chest, his abs, and I pulled down the towel that he had tied on his hips. There was nothing between us, only the hot water that poured down over his shoulders making his skin slippery to my touch.

He kissed down my neck, ran his hands down over my arms.

"I wanted to tell you everything. But I was afraid," I whispered.

He looked at me and held onto my shoulders. "It's okay, Wren. You don't have to be afraid anymore. You don't have to hide. Not with me."

How did he know exactly the right thing to say? There were more words that could come between us, more things I could tell him about how I'd ended up here, or more details of my visions. But we were supposed to be mates. We had forever.

I took his hand and slid it down over my breast.

He squeezed softly and I gasped and leaned into him.

I pulled his head down and this time it was me who claimed him with my kisses, telling him everything I needed to say without speaking another word.

I ran my fingers down his back, and touched his ass. It was a really nice ass.

And then I noticed something new—the scent of fire and cinnamon—Maxwell.

Jace turned around, shielding my body with his.

Maxwell stepped into the stall and sat down on the bench.

CHAPTER 10

It was impossible to tell what Maxwell was thinking. His face was a mask as he leaned his back against the shower wall and folded his hands in his lap.

"Well," he drawled, "it looks like you two are having fun. Please, don't stop on my account."

Nudity wasn't supposed to be an issue with shifters, but I wanted my clothes more than anything. The air felt cold, the hard tile like ice beneath my feet. I grabbed a towel, wrapped it around me, and turned to face Maxwell. "What the hell?"

"I was looking for you," he said. "Followed your scent. Imagine my surprise when it led me here."

My face burned like a dragon's fire. "There was some kind of accident in the women's showers."

Maxwell shrugged. "You don't have to explain anything to me, Wren."

Jace cleared his throat. He'd been quiet until now, and he was still naked next to me. "Wait. Did you say *Wren*?"

"That's her name," Maxwell said, arching an eyebrow. "Didn't you know?"

"I just found out," Jace mumbled, turning a hurt gaze to me.

"I'm sorry," I said. "I tried to tell you sooner…"

"I know," he said, brushing a kiss against my temple.

I hated the pain in his expression, wanted nothing more than to soothe him, show him how important he was to me. But there was the matter of the intruding dragon shifter in front of us. Jace seemed to realize it at the exact moment I did.

"Right," Jace put a hand on my bare shoulder, his touch a warm comfort. He flicked a glance at Maxwell. "So...why are you still here?"

"I don't want to spoil your fun," Maxwell said. "I just...had to see."

"Okay," I said, nerves making my voice shaky. He didn't look mad, but was he just hiding it well? "You've seen."

He nodded and a smile slowly spread across his face. "Yes."

"And you're not pissed?" I asked.

He walked over to me, his dress shoes making small splashing noises in the scattered puddles of water. With a single finger, he traced the line of the towel where it stretched across my chest. "Not at all. I'll let you two finish. Hell, I'll even guard the door. But next time?"

I waited, breath held.

"Next time," he said, "invite me, too."

JACE WAS quiet after Maxwell left. We both dried off and dressed, then I turned to face him.

"I'm sorry I didn't tell you about my name sooner," I said.

"It's okay."

"I can tell it hurt you that Maxwell knew. I actually met

him about a year ago. The Thanksgiving before last. I can't…"

"Hey." He tugged me into his arms. "It's okay."

He ran his hand over my hair, which was still wet and soaking the back of my uniform.

"There's some stuff that happened," I said.

As he held me, I explained my months prior to Spellbound Academy. Being kidnapped and held in captivity by Chad Curtis, the dragons of Emerald Pines freeing me, having Thanksgiving dinner with them. And then my months on the run. Throughout the tale, I could feel Jace's muscles tense occasionally, and I smelled the simmering, rocky scent of his anger.

"Am I making you mad?" I asked.

"No," he said. "Not you. Just everything you've gone through. And I wish I'd known about it so I could make it better."

I grinned and pulled back so I could see his face and he could see mine. "We didn't even know each other then."

His eyebrows were pulled together in a frown. "Still, I'm mad that I wasn't there to help."

"From now on," I said, "we're together. Right?"

"Wren," he whispered, "you're my mate. You have to feel that, right?"

"The others are, too," I said. "Maxwell and Adrien."

"Adrien, huh?" he said.

"Professor Vosovich," I explained.

He frowned. "Isn't he, like, in his thirties or forties?"

"If we're mates, does it matter?" I asked.

He shook his head.

I continued, "I need to talk to all three of you together so we can figure out some kind of understanding. That way I'll know for sure you're all cool with this."

"We're more than cool with this," he said with a little

laugh. "I've been wanting to find you my whole life. Sharing you with two others doesn't diminish that in the slightest."

"Okay, let's all talk."

It didn't take long for us to chase down Maxwell, and he agreed to come with us to Adrien's office.

Thankfully, Adrien was there, sitting at his desk and looking over a stack of papers. Soft music played on an old record player, something with piano and vocals in another language, possibly Russian. He looked up from the papers on his desk and smiled at me. The smile turned to a puzzled frown when he saw Jace and Maxwell.

"Ms. Rose," he said.

"It's okay, Adrien. Jace knows my name now, too."

He exhaled. "Wren. You know how dangerous that is."

"Not when he's my mate."

"I see." He stood and walked over to the three of us. "And I am your mate."

"Yes," I said.

"And me," Maxwell added.

Adrien looked from one of us to another, then tugged me into his arms and pressed a soft kiss against my lips. "Well, then. It seems we're all okay with sharing you. Are you surprised?"

I'd thought I would be, but this felt too right. It wasn't unexpected at all.

It felt like fate.

SOMETHING about that group conversation changed things with me, Jace, Maxwell, and Adrien. As another month went by, I spent time with each of them individually, and they all seemed okay with me being interested in all three—not just as boyfriends, but as mates. It was mind-boggling. I didn't know anyone in my pack who had multiple mates, but since coming to Spellbound, I was learning that it wasn't all that uncommon.

Maxwell held me after Philosophy of Magic. I remained in my seat, watching him, wondering what he had in mind.

Once everyone else was out, he walked over to the door and locked it. Then he sat down in the rolling chair at the desk and patted his lap.

"Ms. Rose," he said in a formal voice. "Have a seat."

After the morning I'd had, I was so ready for Maxwell's particular brand of stern care. Both Prophecy class and Conjuring had been brutal. I climbed onto his lap, smoothing my skirt out so we weren't too far into R-rated territory. He brought his arms around me and I leaned back against his chest, inhaling his scent.

"How's your day going so far?" he asked, running a hand through my hair.

"It *was* hellish," I said, "but now it feels more like heaven."

He helped turn me around and waited, as if afraid to ask for a kiss. Smiling, I leaned over and planted my lips on his. The blinds were drawn, the door was locked, and I had one of my mates, right here, holding me and kissing me like there was nothing more important in the world.

As we kissed, the need inside of me grew. I had his lips and tongue, I had his arms cradling me, but I wanted more. Needed more. Pulling back slightly, I reached for the waistband of his pants and yanked his shirt from it so I could slide my hands under the fabric and feel his too-warm skin. Dragons burned even hotter than the other shapeshifters, I'd learned.

He kissed me again, groaning into my mouth. He cupped my ass with one of his big hands and I felt the searing heat of it. He slid his hand down my thigh and then back up—this time beneath my skirt.

I pulled back to look at him. His features were sharper, everything was brighter through my lust.

Grinning, he said, "I bet I can make the day even better for you."

I could only nod as I felt his hand moving beneath my skirt toward the juncture of my thighs. He traced the edge of my panties, everywhere except where I really needed him, until I was bucking my hips and writhing, trying to make him go where I wanted.

"Do you want that?" he asked.

"Yes," I whispered.

He shoved my panties to the side and then his finger was right there, teasing my clit. I gasped as he pressed it inside of me, then used his thumb on my clit.

I moaned out loud.

"Shh," he said. "We don't want anyone pounding down the door."

He moved his finger and thumb faster, taking me high, so high—up to the heavens, just like he'd promised.

I was soaring and biting my lip to keep from crying out.

Leaning forward, he kissed me, swallowing my moans, licking the bite mark on my lip while I came apart.

His fingers stilled, allowing me to slowly come down, before he pulled them out and put them in his own mouth, licking away my desire.

"Isn't it time for you to get to dinner?" he asked.

I couldn't speak, I could only nod. Leaning forward, I kissed the smug smile on his face and clambered off of his lap.

I was breathless and shaky when I left Maxwell's classroom, and I'd missed most of dinner. I went through the halls in a daze, hoping nobody would call me out on my inattention.

Jace gave me a knowing smirk when he saw me outside of

the dining hall, where I was going to dash in and grab a left-over roll or whatever I could find.

"Is it that obvious?" I asked, smoothing my hair and touching my lips.

"Probably only to me." He laughed, then lowered his voice to the barest whisper. "You have that Ravished Wren look I like so much."

He tugged me toward a closet door, but I shook my head. "I'm going to be late for the extra credit demonstration with Adrien."

"That's already over," Jace said. "Didn't you see the notice? He changed the time. It happened during dinner."

"Crap." I hadn't seen the notice, and I'd missed the start because of my "office hours" with Maxwell. "I need to head down there."

"You know he won't get you in trouble," Jace said.

"He might. He is still technically my teacher."

I turned around, but Jace gripped my wrist and spun me back to him. He pressed a single, bruising kiss on my lips. Desire coursed through me, and I wanted nothing more than to grip him by the shoulders and shove him into the closet so I could have my wicked way with him. But first I had to go see Adrien. Would it be Professor Vosovich who I met, or my mate, Adrien?

With a last, smacking kiss against Jace's lips, I said goodbye to him and headed outside.

Adrien's office was dark when I came through the courtyard, and my heart sank. I'd missed him.

But then movement through the windows caught my eye, and I hurried forward.

"Adrien?"

"Ms. Rose," he said.

Crap. He was in teacher mode.

In a softer voice, though, he murmured, "Wren."

I hurried up to his desk. He was standing in front of it, arms across his chest.

I said, "Sorry, I missed the change in the schedule—"

He stopped me with a kiss. "The demonstration wasn't important. I was worried about you."

"I've been having a space cadet day," I said.

He tugged me closer and wrapped his arms around me. He inhaled deeply. "You smell like a dragon. And a mountain lion."

I felt myself smile as I remembered my time with Maxwell yet again, and a thrill of lust shot through me.

Adrien groaned and I felt his hardness against my stomach.

Feeling naughty, I cupped him in my hand and asked, "Professor, is there any extra credit I can do to make up for missing class?"

He growled and kissed me.

* * *

"Ms. Rose." Chancellor Ellison peered into my Theories of Prophecy class. "I need to speak with you in my office. Immediately."

I would have thought my classmates were too old to make the "ooooh" sound when someone was essentially called to the principal's office...but they weren't. I collected my things to the sound of that chorus and walked into the hallway, looking for the chancellor.

She was already gone, her heels clacking away on the hall floor.

I followed the sound of her footsteps in the direction of her office. What was going on? It didn't make sense that Chancellor Ellison would come to retrieve me herself—she would normally have an assistant do that. Had someone come after me? Was the chancellor going to hand me over? Cold dread filled my belly at the thought of being revealed to the dark forces that had visited my visions.

Or maybe the chancellor had heard of how crappy I was at reading auras. Maybe she was going to preemptively kick me out so I didn't embarrass myself, or worse, the entire academy.

When I reached her office, the door was open. Adrien stood beside it, looking grim. I had a flashback to that day, months ago, when I'd crashed my car into the academy's wards and come up here to beg a place in the school.

"Professor Vosovich," the chancellor barked. "Inside, now. Ms. Solaris, you, too."

I gave Adrien a look, begging him with my eyes to tell me what was going on, but he simply shook his head and stepped into Chancellor Ellison's office.

"Close the door, Ms. Solaris," Ellison said.

I did as she asked and hefted my bag higher on my shoulder before turning back to face her.

"Do you two know why you're here?" she asked.

I looked at Adrien, and my stomach sank. There were only two reasons why she'd call us both here together at the same time. One, someone had discovered me and I needed more security, or two, Adrien and I had been caught.

Chancellor Ellison was disappointed, not fearful.

It was option two. Someone had seen us.

"A disturbing report was brought to me," Chancellor Ellison said. She looked between Adrien and me. "I'm sure you're both aware that teacher-student relationships are against academy policy."

Cora had mentioned it, but I hadn't thought much about it. I hadn't cared.

"She's my mate," Adrien blurted.

"So you say. You have no way of proving it," Chancellor Ellison said.

"You can hear the truth in my words," he said.

She shook her head. "I'm not a shifter; I don't have the gift of sniffing out truths and falsehoods."

The small clock on her desk ticked as quiet stole over the room, Adrien and I absorbing the weight of what she said.

We were in deep shit.

"Besides," she said, "mate or not, I would expect you to maintain a professional, academic relationship with *every* student on this campus, Professor Vosovich. You were seen engaging in intercourse in your office, of all places. This is highly inappropriate and makes me question your placement as a faculty member of this academy."

A muscle twitched in Adrien's neck. He was holding himself still—so still. His fists were clenched at his sides. He was too proud to say anything more in his defense.

"Please," I said, "he's a great teacher—I've learned so much in his class about how to defend myself. The other students have, too. There's just something more between us, something we can't ignore—"

"Ms. Solaris, you may return to your dorm. Your presence here is keeping you safe, and I'm not going to throw you out because of one man's lack of judgment."

"But it isn't just his fault," I said. "If you knew the strength of the mating bond—"

"The strength of this academy's ethical and moral regulations is more important," she snapped. "Professor Vosovich, we need to discuss next steps and a possible dismissal. Ms. Solaris, it is time for you to retire to your dorm. I believe you have a practice exam to study for."

I wanted to be more like Morgan Rose, the girl who was sick of being polite, the girl who wouldn't take any shit. But deep down, I was still Wren Solaris, a pushover despite being the alpha's daughter, and so after one lingering, apologetic glance at Adrien, I left the chancellor's office.

Once outside the door, I leaned against it, trying to catch my breath. How had this even happened? Someone had seen us making love in Adrien's office? The blinds had been closed. No one should've been able to see anything.

But the truth of the matter was, we *had* been together in his office.

Because of me. Teasing him, tempting him, wanting him. If I'd left him alone, he could've kept his own instincts in check.

Tears burned my eyes and I walked back to my room.

CHAPTER 11

Voices carried back and forth, engaging in some kind of debate that I knew I should be listening to. Instead, I sat at my desk in the back of the Philosophy of Magic room and doodled in my notebook. Sunglasses, hard jaws, self-deprecating grins, and wolves—I drew a lot of wolves. Well, if I'd been better at drawing, they'd look like wolves. Mine turned out more like misshapen hippopotamuses with fangs.

The intent was the same, though. I couldn't stop thinking about Adrien. It had been a week, and I hadn't heard anything. There had been a substitute in defense class, and Adrien wasn't in his office. It took all of my willpower to just go to class instead of sitting in his office and waiting for him. There didn't seem to be a point. I couldn't focus anyway.

"Morgan," a girl's voice said.

I perked up at the sound of my fake name. Looking around the room, all eyes were on me. I had no idea what was being asked of me, and I wasn't up for dealing with whatever it was.

"Excuse me." I gathered my books and headed for the door.

Maxwell grabbed my arm at the doorway, stilling me.

"Are you okay, Ms. Rose?" His grip was firm, but his voice was laced with genuine concern.

I looked over his shoulder to the other students who were staring at us. I couldn't do this right now. I couldn't talk to him at all, not after what had happened to Adrien. *I didn't know what happened to Adrien.* "Yeah, great. Personal stuff."

A flicker of something crossed his face. Sadness? Had I hurt him?

"Bathroom," I said, and pulled my arm.

He let me go, and I ran away without looking back. I felt like such a child, running from my problems. But it was for Maxwell's own good if I left some space between us.

It was just for now. Everything would be back to normal soon, and we'd all be fine, the four of us.

I wasn't sure if I believed that, but I wanted to.

I hurried through the hall and raced down the stairs. The walls were oppressing, and I couldn't breathe. I needed air, fresh air. I ran for the door to the herb garden and burst through.

The air was sharp, the cool breeze laced with ice. This spring storm had taken everyone by surprise, but it wasn't unwelcome. I sucked in a lungful of winter, and a chill crossed over me.

Soft flurries fluttered down between the trees, casting the sky in a white glow. A single snowflake landed on my nose and melted on impact. I'd never minded the cold, even without a coat.

There was something peaceful about the snow, like the world was suspended in restful slumber. The forest was quieter, the air felt cleaner, and there wasn't a better place to clear my head than out here.

I walked through the garden, out to the edge of the forest. There was a fallen tree not too far out. Twigs crunched beneath my feet as I walked.

I took a seat on the log and pulled out my notebook and pen.

I traced my finger over one of the crude drawings I'd made of Adrien, over the sunglasses that hid the only part of him that expressed how he truly felt. I wasn't just worried because I didn't know what had happened. I missed him, too.

It was strange going from being completely on my own to feeling so connected to someone, to *three* someones. I'd come to Spellbound Academy alone, but now I couldn't seem to function without all of them being here with me.

I closed my eyes and tilted my face up to the sky. Cold snowflakes tickled my face when they landed. I took in a deep breath and just let myself be, letting go of the expectations I put on myself. I'd thought I had to be the best, had to thrive, had to do everything right to stay here and be safe. But all I really needed was air. Cold, fresh air.

My hair moved, little scrapes on my scalp. My eyes shot open and I shook my head, not knowing what it was. In the back of my mind, panic told me it was a damned big spider.

I scuttled away from the place I was sitting, only to find a set of beady eyes in front of my face. Along with them was blue fur and long, twitching ears.

"Nibbles, you scared me."

The little lapinfée wiggled its tiny bunny nose and made a clicking sound. She looked at me like I should understand, but I had no idea what she was saying. She flew down and settled into my lap. I pet the soft fur on her back.

"Seems like we're friends now, huh?"

She clicked back at me.

"Why is it you keep coming back? Did I do the calling wrong?"

I caught a hint of Jace's dusty scent before I saw or heard any sign of him. So, I wasn't surprised when he spoke.

"You're *too* good at calling," he said. "And Nibbles isn't the only one who doesn't want to leave your side."

"Cute." I smiled at the cheesy line as he slid in beside me on the log.

He planted a soft peck on my cheek. "What are you drawing out here? Nibbles?"

I showed him my notebook.

"Not Nibbles..."

"You can't tell, can you?" I asked.

"Well this one is an animal...a lion? A...rhinoceros? Is it me?"

I cracked a smile. "No."

"The one with the sunglasses has to be V."

I nodded.

"How are you holding up?" He took my hand.

"I'm still here," I said, not sure what else to say.

"I heard you left Philosophy in the middle of class."

"Word gets around quick, doesn't it?"

"Maxwell's worried about you."

"He told you that?"

"No. He slammed me against a whiteboard and demanded answers. He says you're avoiding him."

"That sounds about right. What did you say?"

"I didn't have anything to tell him." Jace's light green eyes sparkled with concern. "Are you avoiding him?"

"I guess I am." I was afraid. I didn't want to say so, but I was terrified the same thing that happened to Adrien could happen to Maxwell, too. I wanted to hide until everything blew over and life went back to normal.

"Because of V?"

He knew. I didn't have to tell him, and he knew. I just looked up at him and he gave me a small, sympathetic smile, before pulling me in to his chest and holding me. I melted into him.

Jace pulled back, and held gently to my arms as he met my gaze. "Are you ready?"

"Ready for what?"

"Exams. We have to head in for your practice exam."

"What?" Panic welled in my throat, and my stomach churned. Practice exams? I'd forgotten all about them. This was like a nightmare, but at least I still had my clothes on. I tried to remember what had been said this week, but it was all a haze.

"You forgot?"

"I guess."

"Come on. It'll be okay, it's just a practice run."

I let him guide me to my feet and we headed back into the school.

There were sounds in the room ahead, loud, bird-like sounds.

Jace kissed my temple and ushered me inside. "Don't worry, you'll do great."

He took a seat, and I did the same. It was a large room with rows of desks. It seemed like everyone from our year was already here already writing and flipping through their test scrolls. I set my belongings under my seat and looked around to figure out where the tests were.

In a flourish of red and orange, a huge, hawk-like bird swooped down and dropped a scroll and quill on my desk. I watched as it flapped its massive wings and returned to a perch at the top center of the room. It stilled and a wash of gold overtook its form, freezing the bird as a statue.

I stared a moment longer before unrolling the scroll in front of me. It was blank, except for a line at the top with the word 'name' beside it. For a moment, I wondered if it was a mistake. Maybe this was a drawing test and I'd missed the instructions. Maybe my copy was misprinted.

Morgan Rose—I wrote my fake name on the space provided. The scroll shimmered, and text appeared in the blank space. It must have been waiting for me to write my name. I wondered if it was the same test for everyone or if they were all different. It didn't matter, not really. I had to focus on answering the questions I was given.

When introducing the ancient precept of "harm none," what was Morgan Le Fay's first approach in her personal writings?

Shit. I could remember looking over the summaries of her writings, but when I tried to picture the text on the page, all I could see were reflective sunglasses.

Stumped on the very first question. This did not bode well.

The next ones weren't any better. Even the subjects I knew I had studied felt completely beyond my grasp. One question after another, and the responses I wrote down were gibberish. My brain felt slow and tired, sadness weighing it down.

I wasn't even sure I'd gotten half of the questions right. After I wrote my final answer, text appeared on its own as the questions had after I'd written my name. But this time it was my score, which turned out to be worse than half. Forty-three percent. *I'd failed.*

After Professor Tiddlywinks collected the tests, I met up with Jace by the door.

"How'd it go?" He leaned a shoulder on the stone wall.

"Not so great."

"I'm sure it's not as bad as you think."

"Worse."

Jace frowned. "At least there's another part. Ready to go?"

"Another part?" I'd barely survived the test, whatever he was talking about had to be better than that.

"The other half of the test, Practical Spells."

"Lead the way." I smiled. Practical spells? At least I'd have this half of the test in the bag. Training with Cora had me above grade level in defensive magic. And after the disaster of my written test, I really needed an easy win.

Jace took me to the courtyard next to Adrien's office. Being here was bittersweet. It should have been Adrien giving this test. I was still expecting him to show up any minute and for everything to go back to the way it was supposed to be. Even so, I was thankful for the guidance he'd given me.

The defense class substitute, Professor O'Leary, called forth three students I didn't know particularly well. Hannah, Meredith, and Joel pushed to the front of the crowd and lined up in front of him.

"For your practical exam, you must summon a lapinfée." O'Leary put his hands behind his back and regarded the students each in turn.

My heart was full, and I couldn't help but smile. Finally something was going right. I could call a lapinfée. Hell, Nibbles showed up even when I wasn't trying to call for her.

"You will be scored on precision of creature called, and temperament of said beast."

I leaned over to Jace to ask what O'Leary was talking about. What did the lapinfée's attitude have to do with anything?

But he looked down to me and whispered first. "Strength of the summoner determines how pissed off the lapinfée is when it arrives. If the summoner can't convince the *lapinfée* to submit to his or her will, then they aren't equipped to call anything else."

I didn't know what else there was to summon. The only magical creatures I'd encountered so far were lapinfées and Guardians. And then there were shifters, but I couldn't imagine a witch being strong enough to call one of us. Who knew what was out there, maybe flying tigers or something. Spellbound Academy had taught me that I knew nothing.

But, I'd rock this test. Nibbles adored me. What did that mean about me? Was she the exception, or did that mean I was strong enough to call a flying tiger?

"Go." Professor O'Leary waved his hand at the three students.

All of them closed their eyes.

A lapinfée appeared first in front of Meredith, then in front of Hannah, too. Joel kept his eyes closed, and his cheeks turned red, but no lapinfée appeared.

"That's enough, Mr. Krell." O'Leary tapped Joel's shoulder.

"But I can do it, I swear. I just—"

"I said that's enough. Return to your quarters and practice. There will be no second chances on true finals." O'Leary raised his voice and addressed the room as Joel disappeared into the crowd. "Let this be a reminder to all of you. Half of you will not make it to second year. If you are not completely competent in all areas, this is your last chance to rectify your position in the standings."

Jace took my hand and squeezed softly. We'd both make it through to the next year. We had to.

O'Leary plucked the speckled lapinfée Meredith had conjured out of the air and flipped it around, inspecting it. The lapinfée was docile, as they always seemed to be.

O'Leary nodded. "Adequate."

He released the lapinfée, and it flew up to the ceiling, seemingly searching for an exit. O'Leary next grabbed the lapinfée Hannah had conjured. When he flipped it over, it twisted in his hands and opened its tiny mouth wider than I thought lapinfées could, and it chomped down on his finger.

O'Leary scowled at Hannah and released the kicking lapin-fée, who flew up to join its friend.

"Inadequate," O'Leary said to Hannah, whose shoulders sank.

Okay, maybe this was going to be harder than I thought. It seemed like she'd passed for sure. But I still had Nibbles. She'd come for me.

"Next will be Jace Gladstone, Morgan Rose, and Devon Browning."

I followed Jace to the center of the room. Devon stood to my other side, keeping his attention ahead. We hadn't interacted since the beginning of the school year, when he'd tried to scare me with the Guardian. No interaction was perfectly fine with me.

O'Leary looked to each of us in turn, and I was just waiting for the signal to call Nibbles. *I could do this.*

"On my mark, you will identify my aura," O'Leary said. "You'll pull from it, and summon an orb of light to match."

Auras? No. Give me calling, please. I could pull from auras, sure, but I couldn't identify one to save my life.

"Go."

"Green," Devon and Jace said in unison. Each held a ball of light in their palms.

I was just standing there. I'd already failed, just like that. I couldn't identify his aura. I scrambled to collect it, willing a piece from it, but O'Leary was already shaking hands with the guys.

"Very good, Mr. Gladstone and Mr. Browning. Next!"

Jace took my hand and led me from the center of the room. I'd failed, not just the written exam, but the practical one, too. How had I let this happen?

Devon smacked his shoulder into mine as he passed and laughed. "Can't believe I thought I needed to scare you away from Spellbound. Or try to get you expelled for fucking

Vosovich. Can't believe that didn't work. But, it's better to have you here. Watching you fail feels so fucking good."

It was him. Devon had been the one who'd told the chancellor about us.

"Fuck off," Jace growled.

I pulled away and headed for my room. All I wanted to do was curl up in my bed. Alone.

CHAPTER 12

I'd failed. *Failed.*

I'd thought to go to my room, but Cora might be there and I didn't want company. So, I walked back to the courtyard, knowing it would be empty at this hour. There, I stood in the cold and looked at Adrien's building.

Everything was coming together to show me that I really didn't belong here. I couldn't do the magic, I couldn't keep my hands off the teachers. Maybe it would be better if I were to leave Spellbound and take my chances in the outside world. Danger and prophecies be damned.

I just wanted to sit in the snow and cry.

I looked around for Nibbles, wishing I had someone cute and warm to make me feel better, but she seemed to have abandoned me.

Get up, Wren, I said to myself. *You're being pathetic.*

But being pathetic felt right. It was fitting for a failure, wasn't it?

There was no way I could get into the top fifty percent of Spellbound students with a performance like what I'd just given in the practice finals. Not with getting fifty-seven percent of the questions wrong. My face felt hot, so I pressed one of my hands to it, needing the coolness.

I knew I could go and find Jace. He'd done wonderfully on his finals. I should give him a kiss of congratulations. But it would also be a kiss of farewell. How would our relationship work next semester if he was here, and I was outside the academy? We wouldn't be able to see each other. I wouldn't be able to see Maxwell, either, if he stayed and kept teaching. If Adrien was out, I could at least be with him. Unless he was so angry about me getting him fired that he didn't want to have anything to do with me anymore.

The thought sent an icy pain in my chest. We were mates. He wouldn't be mad at me forever, would he?

His scent filled my nostrils, forest and wolf shifter, a sensory phantom that I was probably imagining because I missed him so much. Added to that was the sound of footfalls on the snowy courtyard bricks. I held my breath. This couldn't be possible. I shouldn't hope for something so wonderful, so comforting.

"Wren?"

His rough voice came from behind me.

I turned, hardly able to believe it. "Adrien?"

He rushed forward. I held still. He could be angry with me. I deserved his anger.

But he pulled me into his arms in a crushing embrace. "Wren," he whispered. "I've missed you."

"I—" It took me a moment to find my breath. "I missed you, too. Where have you been?"

"Unpaid leave of absence. I'm sorry I couldn't tell you—Ellison made me leave immediately. It's been torment. Every second without you has been torment."

Tears burned my eyes and I pressed my face against his

coat, pulling in the scent of leather and forest. "I thought you would be mad at me. This was all my fault."

"All your fault?" He gave a low, rumbling laugh. "Last I checked, it takes two people to perform the specific things we were doing in my office."

Lust gathered in my lower belly, but I ignored it. "And you're not—you're not fired?"

"No." He shook his head and hugged me tighter. "But we have to...exercise restraint. Ellison spoke to some other shifters, trying to get more of a handle on the shifter mating instinct, and she has a better understanding now. However, we can't do what we've been doing."

"What are the limits?" I asked.

"So you can push them?"

"Maybe," I said with a smile. Then I frowned. "It doesn't matter. I'm not going to pass finals, anyway."

Then a horrible thought came into my head—if Adrien hadn't lost his job, and Maxwell and Jace were still here next year, I would be alone.

He leaned back and gently tilted my face up to his. "What is it, Wren? You just thought of something."

He wasn't wearing his sunglasses, and I could see every emotion in those clear golden-brown eyes.

I shook my head. I didn't want to make him feel bad for keeping his job.

"Tell me," he said.

There was no point in trying to hide it; he'd find out soon enough. "I just...I don't think I'll be able to stay at Spellbound. I failed the practice final. It was...it was horrible. It's going to be hard being away from you, Jace, and Maxwell next semester, that's all."

He gave me a stern look. "First of all, you're not going to fail the finals. No way."

"But you weren't here—you didn't see—"

He shook his head. "And second of all, do you think for a second I would remain at this school, or anywhere, if you weren't with me?"

"But your job," I said.

"It means nothing compared to you. I enjoy this work, Wren, but it holds no power over me. *You* hold power over me."

Standing up on my tiptoes, I kissed him again. My heart felt lighter, freer. I hadn't ruined Adrien's life, he was still here with me, and what was more, he'd be with me no matter what.

I pulled back. "I have to go talk to Maxwell."

"Good idea." Adrien said. "He waylaid me as soon as I returned. Sounds like he's been worried about you."

After giving Adrien another kiss, I squeezed him and turned to go. "You hold power over me, too," I said, then hurried through the courtyard and into the building.

I felt his gaze warming my body the entire way.

* * *

MAXWELL SAT as his desk in his dorm room, studying. He looked up when I knocked on the door jamb. As a TA, he had his own room, although I hadn't been here more than once or twice, and never for long. Faster than I could blink, he was out of his chair and taking my hands in his. "What the hell, Wren?"

I took one of my hands away, reached behind me, and closed the door.

Alone. With Maxwell. His dragon shifter scent filled my nostrils, burnt sky and cinnamon, and I breathed him in.

I could also smell his anger.

"I'm sorry," I whispered.

He dropped my hand and turned away, gripping his hair. "It tore me up that you wouldn't talk to me."

"I thought I was protecting you. When Ellison sent Adrien away, it was my fault."

"Your fault *and* Vosovich's." Maxwell turned around, and his lip twitched.

"And what if she sent you away, too?"

"Wren," he said, stepping closer, "I'm not a professor. I'm a TA. Which means I'm still a student here, and it means I can still have friendships and, yes, relationships with other students."

I poked a finger in his chest. "Not with other students."

"No," he said with a laugh. "With one other student. In particular."

"Does it bother you that you have to share me with Adrien and Jace, but I won't share you?"

He shook his head. "Not in the least. I don't want anyone but you."

"So I can kiss you, as much as I want, and you won't get kicked out of Spellbound?" I asked him.

"Well, maybe we shouldn't repeat what we did in the empty Philosophy of Magic classroom," he said, "but otherwise, yes. Kiss me as much as you want."

I shoved him until the backs of his legs were pressed against his bed, and he sat down.

"Take off your shirt, Wren," he said, his voice a growl.

I toyed with the buttons, my fingers light on the little pearls.

"Don't mess with me," he growled. "I'll rip that shirt right off of you."

I liked the sound of that, so I pretended like the top button was stuck.

"I warned you," he said. Sitting forward, he reached out and grabbed me by the hips and yanked me toward him.

Then he took the collar of my shirt in his fists and yanked. Buttons flew off, plinking against the old hardwood floor. I stood in front of Maxwell with my shirt dangling down my arms. My lacy bra was the only thing between my breasts and his hot, predatory gaze.

"You owe me a shirt," I said.

He laughed and pulled off his t-shirt. Reaching out, he touched the edge of my skirt. "Are you going to take this off for me, or do I have to rip it, too?"

I quickly slid it down my hips. He watched, his blue eyes growing darker. He skimmed the edge of my panties with a single finger, then looked up at my face.

"Do you know how beautiful you are?"

With him gazing at me like that, I felt beautiful, so I nodded.

"Come here." He tugged at my hips again until I straddled him, then he kissed me, all cinnamon and fire. "Don't ever leave me again," he whispered.

"I didn't leave—"

"Not physically," he grumbled. "But in your heart, you created distance. Next time, talk to me. I could've reassured you that we wouldn't get in trouble."

And I would've only been missing Adrien, not both Adrien *and* Maxwell.

"Never again," I said. I'd learned my lesson—days and days of misery.

He kissed me once more, his tongue seeking mine, and I put everything I was feeling into the kiss. No more distance. I gave him affection, love, passion, lust. He groaned into my mouth.

I slid my hands down his chest, exploring the muscles, then all the way to his waistband, where I struggled with the button on his jeans. He let go of my hips to help me, and then, finally, my hand was on his cock, stroking the smooth head and down the shaft.

"I want this in me," I whispered.

"Your wish, my command," he said, reaching for his nightstand. He pulled a condom from the top drawer. Once it was over his cock, he tugged me closer, slid my panties to the side, and waited for me to sink down onto him.

I took my time, relishing the sensation of him slowly filling me. It was agony, going so slow, but I loved it. With my eyes closed, I breathed in the scent of him—dragon, male spice, *Maxwell*. I breathed his name.

Once he was all the way inside, I lifted up and pressed back down again. The friction was delicious, I couldn't get enough. "On my back," I gasped. "I need faster—harder."

He spun us around so that I lay on his bed and he pumped in and out of me, a look of love mixed with desire in his sapphire eyes. I could feel my orgasm approaching, growing, filling me up, until it got too big for my body and it broke and I clenched around Maxwell. A second later, he gasped my name, freezing in place as he pulsed inside of me.

With another kiss, he pulled away and tucked a strand of hair behind my ear. "Feeling better?"

"So much better," I said. "But I have to get going."

His eyes narrowed. "You're not putting distance between us, are you?"

"Nope." I put my clothes on, laughing when I couldn't properly button my shirt.

He got up and rummaged through his dresser. I admired the sight of his bare ass until he finally stood and handed me a sweatshirt to put on.

"What are you doing, then?" he asked. "You could stay here for a while."

"I have to study," I said. "Because no matter what, I'm

staying here at Spellbound for another year, which means I need to kick some magical ass."

A slow grin spread across his face. "Go get your books. You're about to become a master in the Philosophy of Magic."

CHAPTER 13

The next few weeks passed quickly, as I lost myself in my studies. Failing wasn't an option. Lucky for me, I had three men in my life who were just as invested in my success as I was.

Jace was a sure bet with passing the finals in the top fifty percent. His knowledge of Theories of Prophecy was unrivaled except maybe by Devon, and he was definitely in the top fifty percent of the class in Conjuring and Calling. He spent a lot of time studying with me, rewarding me with kisses when I answered questions correctly.

Maxwell had his own exams to study for. The second-year finals were grueling and competitive, just as competitive as first-year finals. They weren't competing for a place at the school, but for careers. I walked past the Philosophy of Magic classroom on my way to lunch one day and overheard Professor Juarez shouting, "This is real life, not some game you play in the forest. Real life! Study as if your careers depend on it, because I guarantee you, they do!" Maxwell must have sensed me walking by, because he gave me a dark, lustful grin that had me skittering away before I could bust into the classroom and jump on him.

Adrien was busier than ever with office hours, extra tutorials, and reassuring panicked first-years. Despite the fact that he and I were observing a strict hands-off policy, he still sent me heated looks that caused desire to pool in my belly.

It was torture trying to concentrate on my studies when all I wanted to do was lounge around in bed, curl up with the guys and get to know them better. Even though we were mates, I still didn't know whether Jace preferred salty foods, or sweet. Conjuring lapinfées didn't seem nearly as important as learning what Maxwell's favorite color was, or Adrien's middle name.

Jace and I were on our way out of Conjuring and Calling when the chancellor's secretary approached me. Her red hair shone in the sun coming through the large windows on the east side of the hallway. "Ms. Rose, I'm glad to have caught you. When you have a moment, the chancellor would like to speak with you."

"Is everything all right?" I asked. I hadn't done anything wrong, had I? Adrien and I hadn't done anything more than talk and flirt, and while Jace and Maxwell didn't share the same restrictions, we hadn't had time for anything beyond the occasional kiss.

Jace squeezed my hand, likely hearing the tremor of fear in my voice.

"Everything's fine," the secretary said, giving me a reassuring smile. "She just wants to discuss some plans with you."

"Okay." I glanced at the grandfather clock at the end of the hall. Twenty minutes until Philosophy of Magic. It would be cutting it close, but it would kill me to sit through class without knowing what the chancellor wanted. "I have a few minutes now."

We walked in silence to the chancellor's office, and the secretary waved me in through the open door.

"Ms. Rose," Chancellor Ellison said, gesturing to a chair. "Make yourself comfortable."

I sat down on the edge. All I could think about was leaving her office in tears last time, when she'd sent Adrien away. This was not a pleasant place. I couldn't make myself comfortable, and my inner wolf felt the same. Yet, I didn't feel any danger.

"How are your studies coming along?" she asked.

"They're going well, I think."

"Excellent. Surely, you've given some thought to your summer plans," she said.

I nodded. "Some."

It wasn't true—I'd barely thought about summer at all. I was too busy trying to keep up with my studies and trying desperately to figure out how to see auras. For an oracle, I wasn't always great about thinking about the future.

Now that she'd brought it up, I did wonder about summer. Everyone left after finals. Where would I go? Could I go home with one of the guys? Having three mates didn't seem so difficult when we all lived on the same campus. Would it even be safe to go with one of them, or would I lead the darkness to them?

If it was this hard to figure out the summer, what would happen in the future? Once Maxwell passed his second-year exams, where would he go?

As if she could read the panic setting in over my face, the chancellor nodded. "I realize there are a lot of forces at play here. I'm assuming it's still too dangerous for you to return home to your parents."

I nodded. With the visions I'd been having and the warning Sparrow had given me, I couldn't risk it.

"Then I would like to offer you a place here for the summer—conditionally."

I met her sympathetic gaze, intrigued. "Yes?"

"You'll be working for your room and board." She walked back to a small door I hadn't noticed behind her desk, and opened it.

I gasped. Giant piles of paperwork towered nearly to the ceiling of the storage area. Some had toppled over, some were crammed into boxes and moldy file folders.

"I realize it isn't an exciting or romantic summer job," the chancellor said.

"I'll take it," I said, gritting my teeth. Options were scarce. At least I'd be safe. The guys all had their own plans, off campus plans. No one was supposed to be allowed to stay. Maybe they'd get a chance to come visit, but I needed to figure out what plans would work best for me. If I could stay on campus, hidden behind the wards, that was it.

"Very well," the chancellor said, looking pleased. "Now all you have to do is pass your finals in the top fifty percent, because your place here is still contingent upon that."

"It's as good as done," I said, but with more confidence than I felt.

THAT NIGHT, I was sitting at my desk, Maxwell was leaning against Cora's because she was out, and Jace was lounging on my bed.

"So, this summer," I said.

"You can come home with me," Jace said, at the same time Maxwell said, "You're staying with me."

I laughed. "I'm staying here, actually. Chancellor Ellison gave me a job."

"You don't need a job for a place to live this summer," Maxwell said. "Just come home with one of us."

I could already imagine them arguing about it—something I hadn't thought about in advance. "No, this place is safest for me, you know that. Maybe you guys will come visit?"

"Of course," Jace said. "You won't be able to keep me away."

"Perhaps we can stay here for the summer, too," Maxwell said.

"That would be great," I said. "But first, I have to pass in the top fifty percent."

"I have no doubt that you will." Maxwell pointed at the notes scattered all over my desk. "You've been studying nonstop."

"You've definitely mastered conjuring," Jace said, standing up to pull me into his arms.

I clung to his thick shoulders. "I hope so."

There were only two more days left. Two more days for last-minute reading. Two more nights where I'd wake up in a cold sweat after dreaming of Devon's gloating face as all the professors in the school pointed at me and shouted, "Failure, failure, failure!"

Maxwell was so silent coming up behind me, that I wouldn't have known he was there except for the hot, hard line of him pressed against my back.

Jace bent his face toward mine and I tilted up, offering him my lips. He kissed me hungrily, his tongue delving into my mouth. He grabbed my ponytail and used it to guide my neck to the side, exposing it to another set of lips—Maxwell's. I gasped as Maxwell scraped his teeth against the line where my neck met my shoulder.

Their heat enveloped me, their hands and lips exploring my body. I was devoured by lust.

"Whoa, whoa, whoa," a female voice said.

I jerked away from the guys' arms and turned to the door, where Cora was standing and holding a hand in front of her eyes.

"What did I tell you about messing around with my brother in here?" she asked.

"Sorry," I squeaked.

She sighed. "Does everyone have their clothes on?"

"Yes," I said indignantly. Although if she'd waited a few more minutes before entering the room, the answer might've been no.

She took her hand away from her face. "Okay, good. This is still my room for another two days, don't forget that."

I hurried over and hugged her. "I know. I'm sorry. I won't have sex with your brother in here until *after* finals are over."

"Ew." But she smiled and hugged me back. "I'm going to miss you."

"I'm going to miss you, too."

Maxwell coughed, and it sounded like the word, "Sappy."

I flipped him off over my shoulder.

Cora laughed. "I see you're not *always* painfully polite."

"Nope. Not anymore. You've taught me well."

"I know I did," she said. "So, other than the insides of each other's mouths, what are you guys studying in here?"

Even though she and Maxwell would graduate in a couple of days, I decided to put it from my mind and focus on how good it felt to be in here with my friend and two of my mates. And I hoped, so hard, that Cora's post-graduation plans with Charlize Geard wouldn't change our friendship.

* * *

EXAM DAY HAD FINALLY ARRIVED. My stomach was a jumbled mass of writhing snakes, each of them suffering from extreme anxiety. Jace and I held hands as we walked to the exam room. Just before we stepped through the doors, Adrien rushed up and stopped in front of us.

The students around us stared, probably because Adrien was gazing at me so intently.

"What's going on?" someone whispered.

"Wre—Morgan," he said. His voice was low, but everyone could hear him. "I love you. Good luck on your exam."

He didn't kiss me, although the look in his beautiful brown eyes said he wanted to. Instead, he took my hand in his and brought it to his lips. I felt his breath against my skin before he let me go, smiled, and walked away.

"It's *true*," someone whispered excitedly as we all filed into the exam room. Rumors had been circulating since Adrien's leave of absence, that he'd messed around with a student. I'd been lucky enough that no student name was attached. The chancellor must have threatened Devon not to give that detail away. I was surprised he'd listened. Now, though, it seemed we were going to be out in the open.

I didn't mind. I wasn't ashamed.

"Yo, Jace, you're okay with that, bro?" a guy called out from across the room. "Your girl is hot for teacher!"

My face burned, but I wasn't embarrassed, just uncomfortable with all of the attention. I'd never be embarrassed by my guys; I refused to let anyone make me feel weird about it.

"Quiet, please," Professor Tiddlywinks called. "Everyone take your seats."

Instead of verbally answering the guy across the room, Jace just nodded and smiled before brushing a kiss against my cheek and finding a seat near me.

I sank into my chair.

The golden bird statue in the center of the room came to life and began distributing quills and scrolls. When mine landed on my desk, I immediately wrote my name on the top line of the scroll.

The first question appeared.

Describe one compelling reason for using deceptive magic, and the ethical considerations involved therein.

I remembered my first day in the Philosophy of Magic classroom, listening to Maxwell discuss deceptive magic with the class.

I could do this.

I answered questions about calling and conjuring, about auras, about the ethics and philosophy of how magic could and should be used.

And then I reached the last question...the hardest one yet.

Are you finished with this exam?

I gripped my quill harder. Was I finished? I went through and checked my answers. Everything sounded right, but was it? Was my description of the steps to call a creature enough, or should I make it longer? My quill hovered over the response.

No. I could have faith in myself, just like I had faith in my guys. I'd chosen right the first time.

I returned to the final question and wrote out, *Yes.*

Instantly, my score appeared in front of my eyes. Ninety-nine percent.

Yes. Yes, I'd done it! If a score like that didn't put me in the top fifty, I didn't know what would.

A smile stretched across my face and I turned to the side to look at Jace. He was smiling at me; he must have finished before me and was waiting for me to finish, too. At the same time, we stood up and carried our scrolls to the front of the room, where we deposited them on the table in front of Professor Tiddlywinks.

"You fucking rocked it, didn't you?" Jace asked once we reached the empty hall.

I grinned and kissed him full on the mouth, then pulled away to say, "Yeah. You?"

He stood up straighter. "Was there ever any doubt about either of us?"

"Nope. But you have to tell me anyway."

"I got one hundred percent."

"I knew you were going to kick ass," I said, kissing him again.

"Now it's time for the practical," he said.

More students were gathering in the hall. As soon as everyone was finished with the written, we'd go to the forest.

* * *

NERVOUS ENERGY LEFT me bouncing in place, fired up and ready to go. One exam down, one left. I'd been practicing. I could do this.

The entire student body made their way from the building out into the forest, weaving between the trees like a school of fish caught in the current. Cora pulled my hand, while Maxwell, Jace, Blake, and Thomas followed behind.

We slowed when we reached a huge clearing. Students were packed together along the perimeter. In the trees behind us were Guardians, lots of Guardians. *Run.* The thought came and went. I didn't need to fear them, because Guardians only went after people who didn't belong here. *I belonged here.*

Chancellor Ellison stood alone in the center of the circle and raised her hand into the air. Excited chatter faded to silence as we waited for her to speak.

"Another year has come and passed, and it's hard to believe it's time to say goodbye so soon." Her voice boomed as if she were using a megaphone. Some kind of magic, to be sure. "Whether you're joining a corporation, fighting for another year at Spellbound Academy, or returning home to determine what your next chapter will be, we're proud of you. Your professors, your families, and your friends are proud. You've come to rely on the relationships around you, relationships that will last a lifetime."

I glanced at Jace and Maxwell beside me, only wishing Adrien could be with us, too.

"You've learned and grown. Now you face your final challenge. May you all perform to the best of your abilities, and may fortune reward your effort." The chancellor lowered her hand, and the students cheered.

A magical darkness filled the forest, leaving the clearing spotlighted by the warm summer sun. Impressive skills, whoever had orchestrated that bit of magic. My money was on the chancellor.

Three people walked toward the chancellor, a dark-haired man and a blond woman in business suits, but it was the third man, wearing all black, who I couldn't take my eyes off of—Adrien.

He turned when he reached Chancellor Ellison, and even with his sunglasses on, I knew he was looking at me. I could feel him all over my skin, and I smiled.

As soon as the chancellor raised her hand, the crowd went silent once more. "Joining me in judging today's performance will be Adrien Vosovich, Professor of Magical Defense; Mr. Jon Majarah from MagiCorp; and from Geard Enterprises, Ms. Charlize Geard."

My breath caught in my throat. Standing beside Adrien was the woman who'd spoken to Cora, Charlize Geard. She was wearing a bee broach. And she was staring right at me.

CHAPTER 14

Geard's eyes narrowed before she scanned the rest of the crowd, only for her gaze to once again linger on me. I tried not to look at her, and as casually as possible moved behind the tall guy who was standing in front of Maxwell.

It had to be my reaction to seeing her that had drawn her interest. If I pretended not to be bothered by her, maybe she would move her interest elsewhere. She was here to help with exams and to recruit second years after all. I was only a first year. I shouldn't be of interest to her.

Still, this feeling in my gut...the vision. The bee meant that *Geard was the darkness*. She was the threat that had put my sister's life in danger, the one that had influenced me to tell Sparrow to stay on the compound. And now Geard was here. For me.

Maybe that wasn't right. I'd spoken to Sparrow, if only briefly, and she was okay. Maybe Geard wasn't here specifically for me, but she was a malevolent force put on my path. What made her the darkness, I didn't know. Maybe she didn't either. If only visions were easier to understand.

"Maxwell Phillips and Cora Gladstone."

Hearing Maxwell's name pulled me from my thoughts and grounded me to the here and now.

He took a step forward and I grabbed his wrist.

"It's my turn," he said.

"Good luck." I kissed his cheek.

He winked at me, his confidence clear. He didn't need luck, but I'd wish it to him anyway.

Maxwell and Cora joined two second years that I didn't recognize, one male, one female, in the center of the clearing with Adrien. Geard and Majarah stepped out to the edge with the chancellor.

The air in front of me rippled, a translucent film rising from the ground and sealing those in the center of the clearing in a stadium-sized dome that appeared to be created of water. I reached a tentative hand forward and poked the surface. It rippled like a pond, but remained firm like glass.

"The dome prevents interference and distraction." Jace leaned close.

"They can't hear us in there?"

"No. It wouldn't be fair if someone out here tried to offer a solution to a friend inside. It also prevents magic from passing through, one way or the other."

"Your test is twofold," Adrien said, his voice booming through the dome as if there were speakers everywhere. "First, you'll need to create a potion. Second, tame the beast."

What beast? There was nothing in the dome besides the students and Adrien.

Barriers shot up from the ground, clear walls encapsulating each of the students in a box. Tables with colored beakers and other alchemy supplies erupted from the ground in the glass cages.

Cora and Maxwell set to work right away, though I had no idea how they knew what to make.

Adrien pinched the air in front of him and pulled, like opening an invisible package that only he could see. Four balls of light rose from his hands and glided through the air to the glass cages. There was a blue one, a red one, a yellow one, and an orange one. They stopped midair, and dropped to the ground.

The blue one grew until it reached up near the ceiling of the dome. It stretched its blue light into a long serpent-like shape, with wings. It looked like a phantom, there and not, like a ghost or echo of a blue dragon. The light grew denser, until it lost its translucent quality, and then it spit water from its massive mouth. The water splashed against Maxwell's box, and his shirt turned the same shade of blue as the spectral dragon. He ignored the beast and kept his focus on the potion he was making.

The red one turned into a huge falcon with long red feathers, and it tried to tear into one of the encasements with claws and beak. The shirt of the guy inside turned red. Yellow became a lapinfée with a horn on its forehead like a unicorn. It grew and grew until it was nearly as large as the dragon, and chewed on the encasement of the girl within.

Each creature must have been chosen for one of the students. I leaned over to Jace who was cheering Cora on. "How is it decided which beast they have to overcome?"

He smiled down at me. "It's a warped mirror of their own essence."

"Warped?"

"Yeah, like Maxwell's a fire-breathing dragon, so he has to face a water dragon."

I looked to the lapinfée and wondered if that would be the same creature I would get, or maybe a wolf instead. And then there was Cora, her light was twisting and turning, like it couldn't decide quite what to become.

"Cora'll get a lion," Jace said. He crossed his arms and watched his sister.

"And these mirror warp things, they aren't dangerous, are they?"

"Not deadly," Jace said. "They disappear if the person they're bound to loses the upper hand."

"And then they fail."

Jace nodded. "Go, Cora!"

I watched the orange light transform, first out like it meant to have wings, then tight again with the face of a lion. Finally it settled on the shape of a lion but with long, feathered wings.

Geard was watching her with a grin, pleased by Cora's progress or her creature. It sounded terrible, even in my head, but I hoped Cora failed. I wished only good things for my friend, and in this case, failing meant she didn't get hired by Charlize Geard. Given the darkness that I had sensed around the woman, not being chosen by her would be for the best.

Maxwell tipped back his potion, drinking every drop of the thick brown liquid. The walls dropped around him and his table disappeared, leaving him locked in with the blue dragon and the other creatures. But only the dragon seemed to notice him.

A pearlescent shimmer rushed across Maxwell's skin, as the dragon spewed an ocean of water at him. A wave splashed against the side of the dome, and I searched for Maxwell in the ten feet of water.

"Fish juice," Jace said.

"What?" I searched unsuccessfully to see anything but dark blue.

"The potion. Maxwell made fish juice. He'll be able to breathe."

I sighed with relief, but what about the others. "What

about Adrien and the rest?"

"The water will stay away from everyone else, but it will try to drown Maxwell. Well, nearly drown him."

That didn't make me feel any better.

A scaled leg thrashed against the side of the dome, right in front of me. Maxwell. He had scales and gills, just like a fish. But how would he tame a dragon?

He swam toward the beast, only to shift into dragon form. Fire and water filled the dome, casting everything in a steamy haze. I watched, waiting, my pulse going a mile a minute, and when it cleared, the dragon was gone and Maxwell was shaking Adrien's hand.

"The first to finish is Maxwell Phillips," Adrien's voice boomed.

A small hole in the dome opened and Maxwell walked out. I watched for him along the side, until I saw the top of his head slowly approaching. Everyone was trying to talk to him, clapping him on the back and shaking his hand, but his gaze was set on me.

I pushed my way over to him and threw my hands around his neck. "You did great."

He lifted me off my feet and kissed me hard. He tasted like mud and fire. I wrinkled my nose.

He pulled back and laughed. "Fish juice tastes terrible."

I smiled. "Yeah. How's Cora doing?"

I turned back and found the red bird disappearing into thin air.

"Finishing second is Kyle Running," Adrien said.

The lapinfée pinned the yellow shirt girl to the ground as it ate her hair. I cringed, wondering if that would be permanent. She screamed, and the lapinfée disappeared.

"Rebecca Kevins has been disqualified," Adrien said.

The walls around Cora dropped, and as the other two left through the same way Maxwell had, it was only Cora and the lion left. She had her potion in hand, something blue with smoke wafting from the top.

She threw it at the lion, who roared with so much force it blew Cora's hair back from her face. Cora fearlessly approached the beast and climbed onto its back. The two flew a lap around the dome before landing in front of Adrien. Everyone cheered. Everyone but Maxwell, who grumbled something about dragons and lions not being an equal challenge.

"Congratulations to Cora Gladstone," Adrien said, and shook her hand before letting her out of the dome.

I started walking again, back to where Jace, Thomas, and Blake had been, figuring she'd join us soon. Other second years were called, and they faced the same test Maxwell and Cora had. If I was lucky, that meant the first years wouldn't end up with a bunch of different exams like we had with the practice round.

After a little while, however, Cora still hadn't come. I considered going to look for her, until I heard the chancellor's voice calling some of the second years by name to come line up with the corporation who wished to recruit them. Maxwell was called to see Mr. Majarah, but he didn't budge.

"You're not going to go talk to him?" Honestly, I hadn't considered that after graduation he might join a corporation. I'd hoped he'd be with me, that he'd be teaching and everything would go on as it had so far.

"I don't want his offer."

I looked up into his blue eyes, and found my answer there in his sharp gaze. I didn't have to ask why, I knew. His place was here, with me, just as mine was with him.

"I have some bad news, though," he said. "Vosovich isn't going to be staying here over the summer."

My shoulders fell and I looked over at Adrien. He was busy congratulating another student. I wondered why he hadn't told me earlier, but I could only guess he hadn't wanted to upset me before my exam. Maxwell, apparently, didn't have the same qualms. I turned back to Maxwell. "Why not?"

"The chancellor thought it best if he took some time off."

"She's a cock-blocker," I said with a snort. "Nothing new there."

Maxwell laughed, but I could sense his disappointment, as strong as mine. He'd wanted me to have company, even if it wasn't him.

Leaning against him, I said, "So I guess I'll be here alone."

"You can always come home with me," Maxwell said.

"And we'd be spending the whole summer looking over our shoulders, worried about danger." I shook my head. "I can't do that to you, or the other guys."

People continued to celebrate around us, reminding me that there was more happening than my internal drama.

"Cora Gladstone," Chancellor Ellison announced, and Cora was already happily standing beside Charlize Geard.

I pushed through the crush of students, trying to reach her, but the crowd was unyielding.

And then first year exams were announced, and I heard Jace's name. I turned to watch as he and Devon walked to the center of the dome along with two other students to meet Majarah in the clearing. Would this be similar to the test Maxwell had faced? Or something completely different?

"Among decoys there will be two prizes." Majarah pulled two silver keys from his pocket. "To pass this final, you must claim one of them."

Devon sneered at the other students. "Best of luck fighting over the second key. You know the first is mine."

The girl beside him was Margaret; she stayed in the room across the hall from Cora and me. She stuck her tongue out at him and gave him the finger. Good for her. Devon was a dick.

"If you don't, you fail," Majarah said.

So that meant only two of the four students in there would pass. It was more of a head-to-head challenge. I wished Jace hadn't gotten stuck with Devon, but I had faith in him. Jace would win, no question.

Lapinfées popped up all around the dome, and the keys in Majarah's hands transformed into lapinfées as well.

"Go," he called.

The students scattered, running through the fluffy storm of cuteness in search of the prizes. Lapinfées flew up and away, clicking and twitching their ears. They seemed to be enjoying the game. The way the students appraised each of the lapinfées, they had to be reading auras to determine which were real creatures and which two were the keys.

Suddenly a sense of dread tightened my chest, squeezing, suffocating. It wasn't related to the task in front of me, though.

I knew even before her hand touched my shoulder that it was the darkness, it was Charlize Geard. Her hand was cold, like steel shackles, and it made my stomach churn.

I turned around, squeezing my fists so hard I thought my fingers would break. I needed composure. I needed to run.

"I wasn't sure when I first saw you." Her voice was as cold as her touch, hidden beneath a false friendliness. "Not until I noticed the way you looked at Mr. Phillips."

Maxwell. What did she know about us, about him? The need to protect my mate was overwhelming. I wanted to growl and warn her to stay away. But that wouldn't help, so instead I clenched my jaw and said nothing. *Tell her nothing. Don't give her anything to use against you.*

"You don't belong in this place, *Wren Solaris.*"

I held my breath, my hands shaking.

"I don't know what you're talking about." I tried to turn, but she grabbed my face and squeezed my cheeks with her fingers.

The wolf inside me boiled at the surface. Fight. Run.

Geard's eyes narrowed as she looked me over. Then a smile crossed her face and she let go. My lungs filled in a rush, the cool air burning like frostbite.

"There's no need to lie to me, girl. I see right through you to the power inside. Come, work for me. I'll pay you handsomely."

"Never."

"Such a pity." She smiled wider, making me shiver. "Your friend will be so disappointed to hear you won't be joining us." Geard pointed across the dome to Cora, whose eyes lit up as she waved at us.

No. I turned back to speak to Geard, to tell her to stay away from Cora, but she was gone. I pushed through the other students, deafened by the sound of my heart trying to beat out of my chest.

A hand clasped around my arm.

I turned, ready to throw a punch, ready to—

Jace. He had a silver key in his hand. The smile slid from his face as he caught my expression. "Are you okay?"

I shook my head. No, I was not okay.

"What's wrong?" he asked.

"Morgan Rose." My fake name boomed, telling me it was my turn in the dome.

"Wren—" Concern marred Jace's sweet face, and I wanted to tell him everything.

People started pulling on my arms, pushing me to the front of the group. I yelled back to Jace, "Find Cora."

That was all I managed before I found myself inside the dome. It was strangely silent inside, disorienting after the noise of the crowd. Three other girls walked toward the center of the ring where Majarah was standing. From somewhere outside the dome, I could feel Geard's attention set on me.

"Same rules as the last round," Majarah said. "Claim a prize or fail."

He held out two keys, which turned into lapinfées. Decoys popped up all around us, but I could hardly focus on anything.

"Go."

Everyone started running, everyone but me.

On the ground up ahead I saw a familiar face with a white spot between her long blue ears. "Nibbles."

She clicked. I took a few steps closer, a voice in the back of my head telling me I didn't have time for this.

But then the sky darkened, black clouds rolling over the blue. The ground began to tremble, gentle at first, then harder. I looked up for Majarah, but he was backing toward the edge of the dome with a terrified look that said he had no idea what was going on.

The ground split, rocks stabbing through the surface in the center of the clearing. There was screaming and crying, but it felt distant. I backed slowly away from the rising rocks that fused together into a humanoid shape. Jagged surfaces smoothed into a familiar menace. *A Guardian.* Of course it was a Guardian, why not? But something about it felt different, felt wrong.

Its skin shimmered and turned from gray to black. It took its first step, breaking off of the rock below. Lapinfées disappeared into thin air, popping away from the threat.

The Guardian howled, and a ball of red energy formed in its hand. The air changed, and everything grew hotter. It lobbed one ball of fire toward me, then another. I ran, avoiding the flame, but just barely.

Fire licked up from the Guardian's hand, engulfing its

entire body.

"What the hell is going on? Turn this off." Majarah banged his fist on the barrier's edge.

The Guardian opened its mouth, and the sound of a voice echoed in my head. "Join me or die."

I knew who had done this, who was controlling this monster. And I knew Geard wouldn't just stop.

"Fuck off." My words felt hollow, given I knew she wasn't really in here. That thing wasn't her, but she'd hear, and she'd know my words were meant for her.

The flames around the creature turned blue and doubled in size. The heat in the dome was too much, it was hard to breathe.

The Guardian threw another ball of fire, this one too hard to avoid. The edge of it hit my leg, and the flames engulfed me. I fell to my knees, my body searing with agony. *Use what happened to you.* At first I didn't know why Professor Thornton's words came to me. When she'd said them, I hadn't understood. Even now, I looked back. So much had happened to me, but none of it was like this. No lesson learned, no grand epiphany.

And then I acted without thinking, and I did what I'd done in the forest by accident the first time. It was my only shot. I pulled from the fire, mirrored the creature's aura, and repelled its magic back onto itself.

The Guardian made a pained, serpentine hissing sound. The fire burning me faded, and it changed from blue to red before disappearing.

The Guardian fell to the ground and its body crumbled to pieces.

I knew the feeling. Everything hurt, hurt so much I could hardly see. Black threatened the edges of my vision as I tried to breathe through the pain. The fire was gone, but my skin burned.

Like a switch, sound seemed to be turned on. Everyone was screaming and cheering. A flood of people surrounded me, and the darkness from the sky faded, leaving it a cloudy blue. I stared up toward the light, the leaves of the trees blurring together as they swayed above.

Just let me rest.

My body was being moved, and my limbs felt like ice, the burn fading only to be replaced by the opposite sensation, too cold. I tried to pull away but I was too weak.

There were hands on me, and I tried to focus. It was Jace, touching my hair softly and whispering something about being okay. It was Maxwell, healing the burns with a soft blue glow around his hands. And it was Adrien, cursing about punishing whoever was responsible. I lay there and gathered strength, strength they lent me by being my support and by being my mates.

When I felt strong enough to try, I started to sit up, only to find Nibbles sitting on my chest. How long had she been there? She made a clicking sound and then flew up into the sky, leaving a large silver key on my chest. I laughed at the absurdity of it. After everything that happened, the key didn't feel so important, and here I was, holding my pass to joining Jace in another year here. Had Nibbles gotten it for me? Just another reason to love that little ball of fluff, as if I needed one more reason. I made a mental note to thank her next time I saw her, and sat up enough to look at what was left of the dead Guardian.

But it wasn't a dead Guardian at all. The stony skin crumbled off to reveal another creature, some kind of imp. Pale skin, black eyes, and what looked like a bee tattoo on the arm, which quickly faded as my eyes locked on it.

The chancellor and professors guided the other students away from the dome, back toward the school. But when I scanned the crowd, there was no sign of Geard...or Cora.

CHAPTER 15

Last night, I'd slept like someone who nearly had her ass handed to her in a magical battle to the death. Somewhat fitful, full of pain, and with a flame-soaked nightmare just to keep things interesting. No surprise that I was waking up late, to the sounds of people packing up.

Across the hall, I heard Margaret crying softly as she packed up her things. Damn my wolf shifter hearing. That was private. I blinked back tears of my own, because for some reason, hearing someone else cry made me want to cry every single time. I'd been that way even as a baby.

Getting up, I found my phone. Here at Spellbound, it was useless for anything except playing music. I put on some soft tunes. Nothing like a little moody Charlie Cunningham to add to the feelings of melancholy. I grinned. Sparrow hated this music—she called it "angsty shit" and she would've been at my phone in a hot second, switching it to some crazy dance beat.

Cora was gone, and our room felt weird without her. The

note she'd left me was still on her desk from where I'd dropped it last night.

I'm going to miss you so much, Morgan/Wren. (Yeah, nice job with the name switcheroo. I get why you did it, don't feel bad.) And stop being so motherfucking polite!

Love, Cora

P.S. Don't have sex with my brother in the bed I slept in. Gross.

I did an experimental stretch, wincing at the soreness in my ribs, but it wasn't nearly as bad as it had been last night. My leg was completely healed, thanks to Maxwell's healing spell.

Margaret's crying had stopped, and I heard her door open across the hall. I didn't know whether I should go out and say goodbye to her, or let her leave quietly. I stood at my closed door, torn, until I heard her walk away. I still didn't know what would've been best. If it had been me, I would've been sneaking out while it was still dark, unable to face everyone. I decided not to chase her down, and let her leave in peace. Her footsteps thumped down the hall and around the corner, until I couldn't hear her anymore.

If I had failed, would she have gotten to stay?

I tried not to think about it. It wouldn't help anything.

As I stood there, I heard Devon's voice. "I'm going to insist on my own room next year. I need to be able to study and maintain my position at the top of the class."

I had no idea who he was talking to. All I knew was that his presence here was nearly unbearable.

Soft footfalls approached my door and I stepped back just as someone knocked. "Wren?"

Jace's voice.

I liked hearing him say my real name instead of my fake one.

Opening the door, I grinned up at him. "Hey. So does everyone know my name, now?"

"Yeah," he said. "It all came out after the final, when Maxwell was healing you. I tried to tell everyone to shut up…"

"It's okay. Charlize Geard knows who I am now, and she's the darkness I have to avoid."

His brow wrinkled. "But...Cora."

"I know," I said. "We'll try to talk to her."

He bent forward and kissed my cheek. "I still have to pack up my stuff. I just wanted to make sure you're coming with us to the bonfire tonight. One last celebration for everyone."

"I'm in," I said, trying to ignore the sorrow punching up through my gut to clog my throat.

One last celebration, until my mates left campus, and I was here alone with the few staff who remained during the summer break.

* * *

TONIGHT'S BONFIRE was even more beautiful than the first one I'd seen out here in the woods. Because tonight, I walked with Jace and Maxwell. Adrien had bowed out, saying it would be best if he didn't come to the "kids' party." I'd called him an old man and laughed when he growled. After Maxwell, Jace, and I celebrated a little while with the other students, we would head back to the school to spend every last second together, before the three of them had to leave.

On the bright side, all three of them would be here with me next year. Jace, because he would be a second year with me. Adrien, because he was a professor. And Maxwell—Maxwell had turned down that fancy corporate job to accept a teaching position here.

Summer would suck, but I could look forward to September.

When we arrived, the kissing game with the ball of light

was already in play. I didn't need or want to kiss anyone except my mates, so Maxwell, Jace, and I hung back. I did want something to drink, though, so I wandered over to the makeshift table someone had set up. It was covered in liquor bottles and grimy shot glasses. I found the three cleanest glasses and started pouring bourbon into each one.

Footsteps disturbed the ground behind me, so I turned to see who it was.

Devon, with a sneer already on his lips.

"Coming over to gloat about something?" I asked. "I'm not interested."

"Just wanted to wish you good luck this summer, freak. Nothing about you is natural, is it? A fake name. A freaky oracle. A wolf witch. And now, what, you have a little harem of weak men to do your job?"

"I'd rather be a freak than an asshole," I said.

Someone behind Devon shouted, and I saw the ball of light sail our way. Devon turned halfway to see what I was looking at.

The ball landed in Devon's hands, didn't change color. He scrambled to get a grip on it, but it bounced away from him.

Right at me.

Once again, I caught the ball.

Once again, my hand burning off would be preferable to kissing the person who'd thrown it. Already, the heat was tingling the skin of my palm. Devon was looking at me with the same horror I felt mirrored on his face. For once, we agreed on something.

Maxwell rushed over, Jace at his side. Maxwell clapped his hands and muttered something. The light in the ball went out, and the pain in my hand ceased immediately.

A few people made sounds of protest, but I stared at Maxwell.

"How'd you do that?" I asked.

"A simple dispersion spell," he said.

I jabbed his chest with my finger. "A simple dispersion spell, huh?"

His grin widened. "Yep."

"Something you could've easily done back in, say, September?"

He laughed, and Jace joined in.

"And miss out on the chance to kiss you?" Maxwell asked. "Nope. Couldn't have done it back then."

I shook my head. "Unbelievable."

Then I looked from the grimy shot glasses and back to my two guys. We were missing someone. Why was I at this party, where Devon tried to ruin things and I kept getting hit by the kissing ball?

"Are you ready to get out of here?" Jace asked.

As always, it seemed like he read my mind.

"Yeah, let's go."

Without even glancing at Devon, I hooked my arms in Jace's and Maxwell's and we walked away.

Instead of leading me to the dorms, Maxwell and Jace walked to the rear of the building, where Adrien's office was.

"What are we doing?" I asked.

"Going somewhere more private," Jace said.

"Whoa, whoa, whoa," I said. "I can't be somewhere private with Adrien. I'll get him in trouble again."

"The semester's over," Adrien said, stepping out of the darkness near his office. "We can celebrate however we want to."

I looked at the three of them. I knew how *I* wanted to celebrate, but would they be down? From the lustful expressions on their faces, it looked like yes, they would be.

"Follow me," Adrien said, going back into the shadows.

I didn't hesitate, even though it was hard to see in the darkness, even with my wolf's vision.

Hidden in the shadows was a stone staircase. We walked up, not speaking, until we reached a door.

"Is this just over your office?" I asked Adrien.

"You didn't think I slept under my desk, did you?" he asked with a smirk.

"I had no idea," I said, "and I was afraid to ask."

"Afraid to ask, why?"

"Because if I knew, I might try to find you."

He growled and shoved open the door, then grabbed me and pulled me into his arms. "I've missed you so much, Wren."

The door slammed shut, and I turned to see Jace and Maxwell both standing next to it, their gazes hot.

"We're going to give you a night to remember us by," Jace said.

"Something to keep you hot during the summer months," Maxwell added.

Adrien didn't speak—he claimed my lips with his.

I gasped into his mouth and felt hands on my stomach, tugging at the bottom of my shirt. I pulled away from Adrien just enough to allow Jace or Maxwell—or both of them—to lift my shirt over my head. Clad only in my bra and jeans, I felt lips and hands everywhere, hot breath skimming my skin, raising goosebumps in its wake. I was carried along on a flowing river of ecstasy, submitting to the love and attention surrounding me.

And yet, I wanted more. My wolf wanted to mark them, claim them as mine, never let them go.

I reached for Adrien's waistband, fumbling with the button. He helped me, unfastening his pants with one hand and freeing his cock. I wrapped my hand around it, loving the silky feel of him.

"How do you see this playing out?" Jace asked between kisses against the back of my neck.

"I don't know," I whispered.

It was our first time all together. I'd given it some thought, but more in a general way. Kissing, touching. Not actual diagrams of who goes—and comes—where.

"We want you to be comfortable," Maxwell said.

"At least, this time," Adrien said with a dark chuckle.

"What do you guys want?" I asked, feeling unsure all of a sudden.

"It's not about what we want," Jace said. "This is about you. You're our mate. Your happiness, your pleasure—that's what gives us pleasure."

I looked at him. "But I want to give you pleasure, too."

"How about this?" Jace said. "I've wanted to taste you, here"—he cupped my sex—"since I met you. You smell so fucking good. Can we start with that?"

I nodded.

Adrien grasped my hand and led me toward a small bed. I hadn't had a chance to look around yet, but as we walked, I noticed it was a studio kind of plan, with the kitchen area, living area, and bedroom area all open. A single rug was the only thing covering the hardwood floor.

Maxwell took one look at the twin bed and pointed to the rug. Jace nodded. "Good call."

Adrien's hands were at my jeans.

"I'm gonna feel weird if I'm the only naked one in here," I said.

Immediately their shirts and pants came off.

"Wow," I said, "that was like magic."

Jace laughed, and Adrien smirked while he reached for my jeans again.

"You know," Adrien said, "you can say no anytime. Even if we're in the middle of things. If it gets to be too much and you want to stop or slow down, just say so."

I couldn't imagine wanting to stop. Already my skin felt

itchy and needy for them, my breasts heavy, ready for their touch. But it was good to know. "Thank you."

"Do you want this?" Maxwell asked, kissing down my shoulder. "Do you want us?"

"Yes," I breathed.

Adrien yanked my pants down, and Maxwell gave me a playful spank on my ass. I yelped and turned an indignant look to him, but he kissed it away until I was moaning and reaching my arms around his neck.

Jace dropped to his knees in front of me, shoving Maxwell's legs until he moved to my side. And then Jace's breath was hot against the front of my panties. My pussy tightened in reaction, eager for his touch. He licked the fabric, and I shuddered, kissing Maxwell harder.

Adrien came around to stand behind me. He pressed his chest against my back. The heat of him—of all of them—was intoxicating.

Jace's mouth was against my panties, kissing and licking me through the lace. I squirmed, wanting more.

Gentle pinches on my nipples caused me to look down. Adrien's hands were on my breasts, and he tugged down the cups of my bra. I moaned as he rolled and tweaked my nipples.

Maxwell continued to kiss my mouth, his lips controlling, demanding. If they kept this up, I was going to come hard and come fast.

"Get out of these panties," Jace said, tugging them down my thighs.

I moved my legs, helping him, and then he lay down on the rug, right beneath me.

"Right here, babe," he said, gripping my thighs.

I lowered until I hovered over his mouth, my legs on either side of his head. Adrien and Maxwell came down to their knees next to me. Were we really doing this? It was too incredible, too good to be true.

Jace's tongue on my pussy was heaven. I wasn't sure if it was because he was a big cat shifter, or what, but his tongue had a slight roughness to it that felt wonderful.

I was already so close.

Maxwell's cock rubbed against my hip. His eyes were half-lidded, blue flames of desire intent on my face. Keeping my gaze locked with his, I kissed down his chest, over the rippling muscles of his abs.

He took in a quick breath and exhaled as I pulled his cock into my mouth. I rolled my tongue around him, loving the smoothness of the skin, the heat, and the burnt cinnamon taste of him.

"Fuck, Wren," he said, his eyes closing briefly before opening again to lock with mine.

"I'm about to," Adrien said with a wry note in his voice. "With her permission, of course."

I pulled away from Maxwell's cock only long enough to say, "You have it."

Adrien's tip nudged my entrance. I was already slippery wet with desire. I leaned back, away from the perfection of Jace's tongue and lips, and Adrien slid in.

So full, so tight, I couldn't move at first. Jace came back to me, turning his head to the side to make more room for Adrien. From the corner of my eye, I looked down the muscular length of his body. He'd wrapped his hand around his own dick. The sight of him pleasuring himself gave me another zing of lust. His fist moved up and down, firm but slow. Behind me, Adrien mimicked that pace, filling me before slowly pulling out. Control. Pleasure.

Maxwell touched my cheeks, reminding me of my full mouth. I ran my tongue along his length, loving his taste, his thickness.

Waves of desire built within me. Jace's mouth was centered on my clit. He sucked and licked in a rhythm that was as frustrating as it was pleasurable. Adrien's thrusts became faster and harder, and Jace had to hold my hips to keep me from shifting away with every one of Adrien's movements.

I smelled the woods of Adrien's wolf, the dusty scent of Jace's lion, and the burnt air of Maxwell's dragon.

Adrien's hands were still on my breasts, and he rolled and pinched my nipples harder. The pleasure continued to build, and I moaned around Maxwell's cock. My ecstasy was reaching a breaking point, and I closed my eyes, seeing all three men at once, feeling all three of them, hot and hard around me, as the feelings within grew too strong.

I tensed and cried out around Maxwell's cock as my orgasm washed through me. Jace came, his release splashing over his abs. Behind me, Adrien growled and gripped my breasts harder, squeezing them as he pulsed within me. And Maxwell wrapped his hand in my hair as he thrust one last time in my mouth before emptying down my throat.

My aftershocks were still rippling through me, so Adrien held me against him, letting me ride them out on his cock. Maxwell and Jace both pulled away, and Jace sat up so he could face me, too.

Once my body had finally recovered, Adrien pulled out of me and kissed my cheek.

"That was even better than I fantasized," I told them.

"Same here," Jace said, leaning forward to kiss me.

Adrien and Maxwell nodded.

"We love you, Wren," Maxwell said.

"We're going to miss you," Adrien said. "More than I can say."

I hated that our first night together was more about

goodbye than about celebrating what we'd found with each other.

"It's one summer," I whispered. "We'll get through it, right?"

Jace reached for me and tugged me into his arms before kissing my forehead. Then he lay back on the rug, holding me against him. I settled my head on his chest.

"Of course we'll get through it," he said. "And imagine the hot sex we're going to have in September."

I stuck my tongue out at him.

"Careful," he said, "or I'll find a use for that tongue."

"She's very good with it," Maxwell said.

I glanced up at him to see that his cock was already semi-hard again.

Eventually, we would go to sleep. I would wake up in a tangle of manly arms and legs before dressing and saying farewell to my men for the summer. But now, though, we had some more loving to do.

CHAPTER 16

Walking out to the edge of campus was bittersweet. It was hard to believe it was over, my first year at Spellbound Academy. I'd made it. More than that, I'd made friends, and found love.

I wasn't ready to give up on Cora, either. She was out there somewhere, with Charlize Geard. Maybe it wasn't even as bad as I'd envisioned. Maybe Geard saved her fire Guardian henchman types for me. But no matter what, I'd never give up until I knew Cora was safe and happy.

Now that it was time for summer break, there was one more thing I needed to do before I said my goodbyes. I needed to check in with my sister, and Adrien, Jace, and Maxwell had agreed to go with me.

Rather than go through the gates at the front of the school, we walked through the forest. Because I wanted to contact Sparrow, I was hoping for more privacy.

I led the three of them to the place where I'd first entered the grounds, to where I'd crashed my car and jacked the wards. My car wasn't there anymore, but I recognized the tree I'd almost hit.

"Here we are. My car was right there." I pointed to the tree.

We were in luck; no one else was around.

"I remember," Adrien said. "I moved it after I brought you in."

I reached out and plucked apart the strings of magic at the barrier. I still didn't know how I could do that. I just could. The guys watched until there was a hole big enough for us to step through, and then they did.

I followed and sat down in the grass. It had been so long since I'd tried to have a vision, instead of one just invading my brain whenever it wanted. I closed my eyes and envisioned Sparrow. I pictured her long black hair and the way she held herself with easy confidence and enough attitude to exhaust our parents.

And just like that, I *Saw* her.

Wherever she was, it was dark, and loud. Bright lights flashed around her as she moved her body to the thudding bass. I reached out for her, and before I could touch her, her attention snapped to me.

Her eyes went wide and she threw herself at me, wrapping me in the ghost of a hug. It was the strangest sensation almost touching her, and made me miss her even more. It had been way too long.

"Wren! *Where are you?"*

"I'm at a magic school. It's a long story," I said. "Sorry I've been out of touch. It was hard to focus before. Then I found a sanctuary to keep me safe, but they have wards that make telepathic communication impossible." With the way this had gone the last time I'd tried, before Spellbound, I was surprised how well this was going now. Maybe I just wasn't afraid anymore. I had every reason to be. Charlize Geard knew who I was, and knew where I was. I should have been more nervous than ever, but I wasn't. Everything I'd learned had made me more confident, and I knew I wasn't alone anymore.

"I'm just glad you're okay," Sparrow said.

The club grew darker, and I knew I was losing her.

I tried to say more, but the loud music made it difficult to talk. My focus was wavering, and the vision was ending.

"I love you," Sparrow said.

"I love you, too."

When I opened my eyes, all three of my guys were standing over me, looking at me.

"Did you reach her?" Jace asked.

"I did."

He offered a hand and I took it, rising again to my feet.

To all three of them, I said, "Thanks for coming with me."

"There's nowhere we'd rather be," Adrien said.

His smile tugged at my heart. It was going to be hard to spend the summer apart, but we'd be together again soon. "I'm going to miss you guys."

Maxwell grabbed my waist and pulled me to his chest, claiming me with his mouth. My body melted against his just in time for him to let go. "This time, don't run off."

I nodded, and he turned and walked away.

"Two months will fly by," Adrien placed his hand on my hip. "You'll be busy, and before you know it we'll return."

"I know."

He put his glasses on the top of his head and kissed me softly. Then he, too, walked away, leaving me with Jace.

"I'm going to miss you," he said, stepping in close.

"Me, too." Sadness welled in my chest. This wasn't a time to be sorrowful. Our life together was just beginning, but it was hard to let go, even for a short time. "What will you do over the summer?"

"Hunt down my sister. If she doesn't call first, I'll be sure to get in touch."

I nodded. "Good."

"And when I return, we'll be second years."

"Yeah," I laughed. "Crazy, right? It feels like just yesterday I was knocking on your door, sent to the wrong room."

"I knew from that moment that you were my mate, Wren. I waited a long time to do anything about it, but I knew. What's another two months?"

"Nothing," I said. Though it didn't feel like nothing. I'd have to stay busy not to miss them like crazy. Given what my time in Spellbound had been like so far, I figured that might not be a problem.

Jace kissed me softly, then he kissed each of my hands before letting go.

I stepped back through the wards, resealed the magic, and watched as my mates walked away.

I heard a clicking sound and a tiny weight landed on my shoulder. I looked over to Nibbles and scratched behind her ear. "Looks like it's just you and me, sister."

Nibbles clattered her teeth and brushed her ears against my cheek.

Two months apart. But forever together.

ABOUT THE AUTHOR

Keyboard ninja, late-blooming bibliophile, proud geek, animal lover, eternal optimist, visual artist.

USA Today Bestselling Author Keira Blackwood writes steamy urban fantasy and paranormal romance full of suspense, action, and a dash of humor. No cheating. Always a happily-ever-after.

www.keirablackwood.com

ABOUT THE AUTHOR

Liza likes her heroes packing muscles and her heroines packing agency. She got her start in romance by sneak-reading her grandma's paperbacks. Now she's a *USA Today* bestselling author and she spends her time writing about hot shifters with fierce hearts.

FREE BOOKS—Join Liza's mailing list and get Fierce Heartbreaker for FREE, as well as an exclusive Sierra Pride prequel story and more fun bonuses! Go to Liza's Free Book page to get started: https://lizastreetauthor.com/free-book

Printed in the USA
CPSIA information can be obtained
at www.ICGtesting.com
LVHW050955220624
783734LV00009B/495